THE HERO SHE NEEDS

UNBROKEN HEROES
BOOK 1

ANNA HACKETT

The Hero She Needs

Published by Anna Hackett

Copyright 2023 by Anna Hackett

Cover by Hang Le Designs

Cover image by Wander Aguiar

Edits by Tanya Saari

ISBN (ebook): 978-1-923134-00-3

ISBN (paperback): 978-1-923134-01-0

CHAPTER ONE

She didn't want to die.

"Oh, my God. Oh, my God." Gemma had no idea where she was. Her head was fuzzy, and she couldn't think.

She slapped some branches out of her way, running as fast as she could.

Darting between some trees, she ignored the pain in her bare feet. She'd stepped on something, and cut herself. Where were her shoes? Panic and fear hit her like bricks.

She had no shoes on.

She didn't know where she was.

And someone—several someones—were chasing her.

Air sawed in and out of her lungs. She looked around. Nothing but trees as far as she could see. She sagged briefly against a tree trunk, trying to catch her breath. Trying to think.

In the distance, she heard shouts.

They were looking for her.

Hunting her.

Fighting back a sob, she pushed off the rough bark and kept running.

"I'm not going to die." She bit her lip. "I'm *not* going to die."

Her head throbbed with every beat of her heart. She couldn't remember anything. It was like there was fog wrapped around her memories, filling her head, obscuring her thoughts. And she was so thirsty.

More shouts.

Keep moving, Gemma.

She had to find a way out of these trees. No one would be coming to help her. She frowned. Her family...

God, she couldn't remember them. Why was she so sure they wouldn't be looking for her?

Suddenly, she tripped and slammed into the ground. The air rushed out of her lungs, and she whimpered.

Despair wrapped around her like rope.

She was so alone.

"Get up, Gemma." She pressed her hands to the rotting leaves on the damp ground. "Get up."

She pushed to her feet, and the world swam drunkenly. There were colored leaves all around her, which, if she wasn't running for her life, she'd think were gorgeous. She turned her head, trying to find a path, but everything became a whirl.

She sure wasn't in LA anymore. She rubbed her forehead. That was home. Her heart thumped against her chest. She should be in LA.

This damn forest wasn't home. Or were they woods?

Wait, what was the difference between a forest and woods, anyway?

She bit back a whimper and shook her head. *Focus, Gemma.*

A twig snapped nearby.

Close.

Too close.

Her already laboring heart lodged in her throat, her pulse thundering in her ears. She took off running.

"She's over here!" a man yelled.

No. *No.*

Fueled by fear, she ran faster. Branches hit her face and body, her breathing sawing in and out in frantic gasps. Running was not something she did often, she remembered that.

If she made it out of this, she'd swap a few yoga sessions and lattes for running and green smoothies.

All of a sudden, a man dressed in black appeared to her left from behind a tree.

She gasped. It was one of them. Black cargo pants, hard face, mean eyes.

"You have nowhere to go." His voice sounded like gravel. "We'll drag you back to the car, and I'll make sure you don't get free of your ropes again."

Dizziness hit and Gemma bumped into a tree.

The man smiled. "The drug is still slowing you down. Just give up. You aren't getting away."

She stepped back, and a stick crunched under her bare foot.

She looked down. It was a decent-sized stick, with a sharp point on the end.

As her captor advanced, she crouched, and her fingers closed around the wood. She'd learned that you didn't always get what you wanted from life, but the chances increased if you took action yourself.

When you fought for yourself.

With a grunt, she surged upward, swinging the stick.

Right into the asshole's face.

"Fuck!"

He toppled backward, and Gemma leaped over him. She took off running again.

She didn't stop. She didn't look back.

Her heartbeat echoed in her head.

Run. Escape. Run.

She heard water running nearby and tilted her head. A river, maybe?

A gunshot echoed through the trees.

With a garbled cry, she took off like a sprinter. She raced through some more damn trees, then she tripped once again. She hit the ground hard.

Pain throbbing through her, she tried to regroup. Were they going to shoot her? Her vision swam, her fingers digging into the dirt.

She needed a plan, but her head was too heavy. It was too hard to think.

She was a baker, for God's sake. Her best skills were caramelizing sugar and making perfect macarons. Not self-defense or hand-to-hand combat.

Just keep moving.

That, she could manage.

Pushing to her feet, she took off at a jog. Her left leg hurt now, and she was half limping. There were more

THE HERO SHE NEEDS

gunshots, and she flinched. Raised voices echoed through the trees.

Were they getting closer?

A sob tried to escape her, but her chest was too tight, her heart was racing too fast.

"Found her trail," a man yelled. "This way!"

No. She bit her lip hard enough that she tasted blood, but she ignored it and pushed for more speed.

How much longer could she keep running?

Gemma shoved through some more trees...and came out at the edge of a river.

Oh, God.

One second the ground and trees were right there, and the next, her foot hit nothing but air.

She windmilled her arms, trying to stop her momentum. She had a brief moment to take in the tree-lined river and all the colorful leaves, then she was tumbling down the riverbank.

She might've screamed, she wasn't sure. Something hit her head, and pain exploded through her skull.

She hit the water. It was a shock of cold.

After that, there was nothing but blackness.

"OKAY, YOU STAY IN THE TRUCK." Boone Hendrix turned off the engine and pulled out his keys. "I won't be long."

A low whine sounded from the seat beside him.

He turned to face his dog.

"I'll be quicker by myself. We only need a few things.

If you come, you have to flirt with everyone and explore. I want to get home so we can maybe do a bit of fishing before it gets dark."

Atlas, his German Shepherd, whined again and edged closer. He butted his head against Boone's side.

Boone let out a gusty sigh. "Fine."

Atlas lifted his handsome head, his tail wagging.

"Manipulative, you are." Boone opened the door and slid out. He held it as Atlas jumped down.

The German Shepherd was big, fit, and well-trained. He'd worked as a military dog until his handler had been killed in combat. Atlas hadn't coped well and couldn't go back to work.

Boone understood that feeling.

Atlas had come into his life just as Boone had left the military. When an Army friend had called, asking if he was interested in a dog, he'd said no. At the time, he hadn't been interested in anything.

But he sure as hell hadn't been able to let a dog—who'd served his country, no less—be put down.

So here he was, several years later, getting bossed around by the big furball. His boots crunched on the gravel as he walked toward the stone building that housed the local general store.

Haven, Vermont was tiny. It had one café, one hardware store, an auto shop, and the general store that sold a little bit of everything. That was about it. The best thing was that there weren't too many people, and there were no reasons for tourists to venture this way.

It was a pleasant fall afternoon. It wasn't too cold yet, but the evenings were starting to get chilly. Last night,

Atlas had snuck into Boone's bed. Something the spoiled dog tended to do in winter.

Boone pushed open the door, and a bell rang. The store was filled with shelves. There was a display of some baskets up front by the counter, filled with local produce. This time of year, it was pumpkins and apples.

An older man sauntered out of the back room. "Boone. How ya doing?"

"Good, Frank. Just needed some bread and milk."

The man nodded.

"Is that Boone? Did he bring my one true love?" A woman bustled out, a frizz of gray curls around her makeup-free face.

"I thought I was your one and only true love," Frank grumbled.

"Sure, sure." May patted Frank's arm absently as she skirted the counter. Her face lit up. "There he is. Atlas. As handsome as ever."

Boone's dog bounded over to shamelessly lap up the pats and affection. Boone rolled his eyes and went to grab the things he needed. He set them on the counter as Frank rang them up.

"Boone, I baked some bran muffins today." May held up a plate. "Want one?"

He didn't need Frank's quick head shake—out of view of his wife—as a warning. Boone had already learned that May was a terrible cook. Her baked goods might look okay, but they tasted horrible.

"No, thanks, May. I'm fine."

"You can't be watching your figure." Her gaze

scanned Boone's body. "You haven't got a lick of fat on you."

He might've left the military, but he still did a few freelance jobs. It meant he had to keep in shape. He ran, worked out, and chopped a lot of wood. Sometimes, in the middle of the night, when the demons didn't let him sleep, swinging an axe was the only thing that helped.

"I'm good, thanks."

"Suit yourself." She grabbed a muffin. "Atlas, I bet you'd like a treat."

Oh, Boone's dog loved treats, but he wasn't dumb. He'd learned his lesson as well.

Atlas quickly padded in behind Boone.

Coward. Boone rubbed the top of the dog's head. "Ah, I fed him a little while ago." He handed his credit card to Frank.

May huffed out a breath. "No one will humor an old woman."

Frank grunted. "Everyone wants to keep their teeth and stomach lining intact."

"Francis Harris."

Frank circled the counter and slid an arm around his wife. "You have other skills. I didn't marry you for your cooking."

May's wrinkled face softened.

"Which is lucky for you," Frank continued. "Or you'd be an old spinster."

May elbowed her husband.

"I'll see you two later." Boone grabbed the paper bag and headed out of the store.

He didn't know many couples like Frank and May,

committed for so long. They clearly loved each other, flaws and all. He knew relationships worked for some people, but he figured there had to be a whole hell of a lot of luck involved.

He reached his truck. Relationships weren't for him. Opening up, trusting, sharing. No, he preferred being alone.

There'd be no one to see the jagged mess of his soul. To wake up with his nightmares. To look at him with confusion and pity.

Learn to like being alone, son. It's the best advice I can give you.

His uncle's voice echoed in his head. The old, cantankerous bastard had raised him after Boone's parents had been killed when he was twelve. Uncle Ben had never married. He'd been a loner, through and through.

Boone whistled for Atlas, who was sniffing around the truck's tires. The dog leaped inside.

Sliding in, Boone started the truck and headed for home.

As he drove down the winding road back to the farm, he took a moment to admire the leaves and all the colors. He had to admit that he loved fall in Vermont. He turned onto his gravel driveway.

Beyond the drive there lay rolling, green fields, and patches of thick trees. He pulled up in front of the cabin.

There was a larger building farther down the driveway. He'd boarded up most of the windows to keep the critters out. The main house was too big for him, and needed a lot of renovation—new plumbing and electrical, to start. His uncle had never bothered with it after he'd bought the farm.

Boone climbed out and grabbed his shopping bag. Atlas leaped down and headed for the smaller groundskeeper's cabin. It was a one-bedroom, cozier and a lot more rustic. It had been Uncle Ben's place and now it was perfect for Boone. The structure also had a small loft that had once been where Boone had slept as a kid. Now, it was where he stored his books, but Atlas had also claimed it. His dog bed—that he didn't always use—dominated the space.

Boone passed the woodpile, eyeing his axe stuck in a log. Soon, he'd be lighting fires every night. He had plenty of logs split, but he always prepared extra, just in case.

Look at you. Farm, dog, firewood. You came home to your cozy farm, but the others didn't. Miles, Charlie, Julio. They had kids, wives, families.

You have nothing.

You should've died, not them.

The muscles in his jaw tightened. That ugly voice always whispered to him. Intruding when he least expected it.

Dragging in a deep breath, Boone opened the cabin door. He dropped the groceries in the kitchen and put the milk in the fridge.

The walls seemed to close in.

He'd just had a job in Louisiana recently, working personal protection for a wealthy businessman. He hadn't planned another one, but maybe he should.

"Fuck." He stomped out of the cabin. He had to get out.

Outside, the air was cool and fresh, and his pulse settled a little. He used the breathing techniques that he'd learned to calm himself down.

Scraping a hand through his hair, he whistled, and Atlas appeared. Like his dog knew, Atlas brushed against Boone's leg.

"There are a few hours of light left." He gave the dog's head a scratch. "How about we go fishing?"

Atlas gave a low woof.

Boone grabbed his fishing gear from the mudroom and headed for the river.

CHAPTER TWO

B oone tossed his line in the river and breathed deeply.

He smelled water and trees and could feel himself relaxing. Even as a grieving boy, he'd loved Vermont. His uncle hadn't known what to do with a sad, angry twelve-year-old boy, but he'd had land where Boone could run wild.

When his uncle had died of cancer a few years back, he'd left the farm to Boone.

It had given him a place to come home to after he'd left the military.

Nearby, Atlas was exploring the edge of the river, where the water gurgled over rocks. Then the dog lifted his head, his gaze zeroed in on the nearby bushes.

Boone fought a smile. Atlas loved chasing squirrels.

The fish didn't seem interested in biting this afternoon, but he didn't care. Just being outside, doing something, helped him stay level. It wasn't many people's idea of a fun Friday night, but it suited him just fine.

He might grill this evening. Atlas loved a juicy steak.

Suddenly, he saw Atlas go on alert.

Frowning, Boone watched the dog as he walked right to the edge of the water.

"What is it, boy?"

Atlas kept staring at the water, then he started barking. Deep, resonant barks that echoed through the trees.

Boone's gaze narrowed, and he scanned the far riverbank. He didn't see any movement, and couldn't spot anything out of place.

But Atlas didn't bark for no good reason. He was too well trained. The dog barked again, and Boone started reeling in his line.

"Atlas, what can you sense?" He often wished his dog could talk. The line snagged on something. His head jerked up, then his muscles went tight.

There was someone in the water.

Correction. There was a *woman* in the water.

Moving on autopilot, Boone kicked his boots off and waded in. Once it was deep enough, he dived into the river.

Fuck. The water was cold.

But he'd been part of Delta Force. A Delta operator never let the heat or cold bother him. He hadn't been a Navy SEAL, but later, as a part of Ghost Ops, he'd worked beside some of the best SEALs in the world. They'd taught him a few things.

Boone sliced through the water, ignoring the temperature. His brain clicked into mission mode. He blocked out the physical discomfort and focused on his mission objective.

The current was swift, but manageable. The woman was being tossed around by the water. Shit, was she still alive?

He reached her and hauled her to him, pulling her onto her back. He yanked the fishing hook free of her hair, then started back toward the bank. Atlas stood at attention, his body alert and tense.

Boone's feet touched the rocky bottom, and he stood, then he hauled the woman into his arms. She was a sodden dead weight.

Damn. Please be alive.

He strode out of the water and dropped to his knees on the grass. He laid her out, and got the impression of tangled dark hair, and a scatter of freckles on pale, pale skin.

He pressed a palm to her chest, then he let out a sharp breath. She was breathing.

"Hey, can you hear me?" He pressed two fingers to the side of her neck and felt a fluttering pulse against his fingers.

Thank fuck.

"Time to open those eyes." Gently, he patted down her body, searching for any serious injuries. She was small and curvy. There were no obvious injuries, except that her feet were bare and scratched up.

He frowned. What the hell had happened to her? Where had she come from?

That's when he noted the faint abrasions on her wrists. *Hell.* Had she been tied up?

Atlas sat close and whined.

"She'll be all right, buddy. We'll make sure of it."

He pushed her hair off her face. She had a nasty bump at the base of her skull. She'd hit her head on something.

"Okay, sleeping beauty. Wake up." Her skin was cold. The water was icy, and he had no idea how long she'd been in it. Hypothermia was a risk.

Suddenly, the woman moaned and reared up. Her eyes opened.

Boone stilled. Her eyes were hazel. Green with gold flecks.

Oh, fuck. He knew her.

He'd seen her face on the television, and in news articles, when she'd been pictured with her father.

It wasn't every day Boone fished a billionaire heiress out of the river.

Gemma Newhouse was the daughter of the richest man in America.

Shit. Boone smelled trouble. The bad kind.

"Who—?" She coughed, then turned to the side and vomited up river water.

"There you go." He touched her back.

"*God.*" She sucked in a breath, awareness seeping a little into her hazy eyes. "Who are you?" She tried to scramble backward. "Leave me alone!"

Boone held out a hand. "I'm not going to hurt you. I just pulled you out of the river."

"River?" Her brow wrinkled. She touched the side of her head and looked confused. "I can't think."

"What happened to you? Did you fall into the river?"

"I...I'm not sure." She rubbed her temples. "People

were chasing me. I ran." Atlas whined, and Gemma jolted, staring at the dog. "Oh."

"He's friendly."

"Hi." She held out a shaky hand and Atlas licked it.

Boone saw a faint flicker of a smile on her lips. "This is Atlas. He's a huge flirt."

She swallowed and looked nervous.

He kept his tone friendly and even. "Gemma, I'm Boone."

She tensed. "You know my name."

"I think most of the country knows your name. One, because of your father."

Her nose wrinkled. "Is there a two?"

"Yes." Boone cleared his throat. "Atlas likes watching *Cake and Bake*."

She'd been a contestant on the popular reality baking show.

Her eyebrows winged up. "Really? Your dog watches TV?"

"Really. He loves it. Now, let's get you to the hospital."

Her arm snapped out, and she gripped his wrist. "*No*."

Boone paused. "I—"

"*No*." Her voice was a frantic whisper. "They'll find me."

HEAD STILL FOGGY AND THROBBING, Gemma tried to think straight.

It was hard to do with fear choking her. She shivered. And when she was frozen. She felt like her insides had turned to ice.

Blinking, she focused on her rescuer.

Her heart thumped. Her gruff, handsome rescuer.

Apparently, her brain wasn't so cold and scared that it couldn't appreciate a hot guy. Her stomach did a sickening turn. Could she trust him, though?

She wrapped her arms around her middle. She felt so alone. She had no idea what to do.

"Come on," Boone said. "Let's start by getting you out of those wet clothes and warmed up."

Boone—boy, the name suited him. He had a mountain-man vibe, but he also reminded her of Captain America. Tall, muscled, steady, a superhero ready to save the world. His eyes were golden brown, and looked like they assessed everything.

What if he sells you out to the men who are hunting you?

She bit her lip. One thing she'd learned having a really wealthy father was that money motivated people to do terrible things. It turned generally honest, normal people into greedy, horrible people. She'd had friends betray her. Try to steal from her. People befriend her just to try to get closer to her father and his billions.

Boone's dog Atlas bumped his head against her shoulder.

She patted the dog, admiring his black and tan coloring. Surely a man who had such a gorgeous dog couldn't be bad? She met Boone's gaze. He looked back steadily. Then she nodded.

He helped her sit up, and she saw the muscles in his arms flex. His flannel shirt was rolled up to his elbows, showing off a pair of muscled forearms. One was covered in black ink. She'd never had a thing for mountain men before, but she was starting to see the appeal.

Her head throbbed. God, she was losing her mind. Her life was in danger and she was staring at a stranger's arms.

"Gemma?"

She focused back on him. He was holding out a hand to her.

She placed a palm on his. His fingers were warm and strong. He pulled her to her feet.

The world wobbled. She wasn't as steady as she'd hoped. She gritted her teeth. She was done being helpless and afraid. A huge shiver wracked her, and she tried to take a step.

And collapsed.

Strong arms caught her and lifted her off her feet. *God.* She squeezed her eyes closed as dizziness washed over her.

"Sorry," she whispered.

"Nothing to be sorry about." He let out a whistle, and Atlas bounded ahead of them.

Then he strode across the grass.

Gemma had no strength left. She dropped her head to Boone's shoulder. His clothes were wet too, but she could feel the heat radiating off him.

"I'm heavy." She had curves. Curves her mother was always telling her to work off.

Boone snorted. "No, you're not."

He didn't appear to have trouble carrying her. She felt a little flutter in her belly. Then suddenly the cold clamped on to her and wouldn't let go. She couldn't stop the shivers. Her bones felt cold. Her teeth chattered.

"B-Boone..."

"Hold on, Gemma. We'll get you warm. My cabin is close by."

Her vision blurred, and she just held onto him.

Were those men still after her? Would they find her? Another violent shiver hit her, and she closed her eyes. She didn't have any energy left.

"Gemma, stay awake. Look at me."

She tried, but her eyelids were too heavy.

"*Gemma.*"

He had a nice voice. Deep, resonant. Even through her wet clothes, she felt the heat of him. He was big, strong, and warm.

But then consciousness leaked away, and the darkness swallowed her again.

FUCK.

Gemma turned into deadweight in Boone's arms.

She had been talking, lucid. Was she hurt worse than he'd thought? He hurried toward the cabin, Atlas keeping pace beside him.

When he reached it, he kicked the door open. Getting her warm was his first priority. He'd seen hypothermia kill before.

He set Gemma on his couch. Atlas made a sound. Boone knew the dog was worried.

"I know, boy. We'll get her warm. We'll take care of her."

Her wet clothes needed to come off first.

With some maneuvering, he got her wet pants off and uncovered slim, pale legs and soft thighs. Boone's mouth firmed and he forced his gaze away.

She's hurt, you asshole.

He methodically got her shirt off. *Hell.* Her bra and panties were pale blue. He turned away and grabbed the throw blanket off the back of his couch. He wrapped her in it, then without looking, got her wet underwear off.

It wasn't easy trying to work under the blanket, but soon she was naked. He blew out a breath, then went to light the fire. He already had a box full of cut logs.

He got the fire going and noted that Atlas had stayed sitting beside Gemma.

"Good boy. Keep an eye on her while I change."

It was a relief to get out of his wet clothes. He pulled on a clean set of jeans and a gray T-shirt. He also grabbed another blanket off his bed.

When he got back to the couch, Gemma hadn't moved. Her eyelashes were inky dark against her skin. She had the cutest freckles across the bridge of her nose.

She was still shivering.

He spread the second blanket over her, then sat down beside her and pulled her closer. "You're safe now."

But her shivering got worse. *Shit.* Quickly, Boone pulled off his shirt, then pulled her onto his lap.

She half turned and mumbled something before she

burrowed into him. He tucked the blanket securely around the both of them.

"Come on, Gemma. Open those eyes." He smoothed a hand down her hair. "Come on."

They opened slowly, but her gaze wasn't focused.

"You hurt?"

She blinked. "Drugs. They...drugs." Her eyes closed again.

Shit. Whoever had snatched her had drugged her. Anger seared through him. The assholes. He touched her abraded wrist. Drugged *and* restrained.

His gut tightened. She needed to get checked by a doctor.

"Gemma, you need the hospital."

"No. *No.*" She thrashed around.

Dammit. "Okay, okay." Part of him was filled with the fierce urge to keep her safe, to calm her fear.

Who the hell would hurt a woman? Especially one with delicate features and skin that looks so smooth and soft.

Hendrix, focus.

He fumbled to reach his cellphone, then scrolled through until he found the contact he wanted.

It rang and rang.

"Come on, Rex."

Finally, it connected.

"What?" a deep voice growled.

"I need your help."

There was a pause. "Atlas all right?"

"He's fine. Rex, bring your bag, and don't rush. Just act normal, like you're coming for a regular visit."

There was another pause. "Fine. I'm coming."

Boone glanced out the window. Gemma can't have been in the river too long. It was clear she'd escaped someone.

So where were her captors?

And were they still looking for her?

He tightened his grip on her.

"No one's going to hurt you."

CHAPTER THREE

H e was holding Gemma tight when he heard the crunch of tires on gravel. He knew the rumble of Rex's truck, but he wasn't taking any chances.

Boone settled Gemma on the couch. She didn't move or make a sound. He tucked the blanket more securely around her.

Atlas was sitting as close to the couch as he could.

"Stay close, Atlas. Protect her." Boone patted Atlas on the head, then nabbed his Glock 19 off the side table.

He strode to the window, scanning outside through the curtains. He spotted Rex's battered red truck and the man circling it. Boone met his uncle's friend at the door.

Rex grunted. "What's the emergency? And what's with all the cloak-and-dagger?"

"Come in." Boone was used to Rex's gravelly voice and gruff demeanor.

The man wasn't tall, but he was still in shape—with broad shoulders, and a barrel chest covered by a red-flannel shirt. His hair was gray and buzzed short. He was carrying his black leather bag. He and Boone's Uncle Ben had served together in the Army.

"You can't tell anyone about this."

Rex's bushy eyebrows drew together. "About what?"

"Her." Boone walked over to the couch and crouched beside Gemma. Her hair was dry now, and a lush chestnut brown. He wanted to touch her, but instead curled his fingers into his palm.

Rex just stared. "Did you kidnap her?"

"What? No. Of course not." *Fuck.* "I found her in the river. Hurt."

Rex's frown deepened, and he dropped his bag on the wooden coffee table, then gave Atlas an absent pat.

"She said she'd been kidnapped. She escaped, but they were after her. She was cold, scratched up, and out of it. She also said they'd drugged her."

Rex cursed and checked her pulse.

"She's been tied up, Rex."

The older man made an angry sound, pulling out a stethoscope. "She should be at the hospital. You call the sheriff?"

Boone shifted uncomfortably. "She begged me not to take her to the hospital."

"She was conscious? Talking?"

Boone nodded. "She knew her name, but she couldn't remember her most recent memories. She didn't know exactly how she got into the river, or who was after her."

Rex grunted. "You trust her story? This isn't some weird ploy to rob you blind?"

"Yes, I trust her. Trust me, she doesn't need my money. She's kind of famous, Rex."

"She is?" The man eyed Gemma's face, then he shrugged. "You know I don't have a TV."

"Someone's after her. Her father's wealthy."

Rex's face hardened. Like Boone, he was a man who wouldn't stand for seeing innocent women hurt.

"She'll be fine. Her pulse is strong. The drug is clearly working its way out of her system. I don't see any sign of any adverse reaction, but you need to watch her. Keep the fluids up, give her some food when she wakes up."

"Got it."

"She's pretty scratched up. Feet copped the worst of it. Risk of infection."

Boone swallowed. "Leave me some stuff, and I'll clean and bandage her injuries."

Rex eyed him for a second, then nodded. He pulled out bandages, antiseptic wipes, and cream. "What's your plan, boy?"

Boone shrugged. "Keep her safe. I'll give my old commander a call. He runs a security company."

Rex nodded. "What if you get visitors?"

"You know I can take care of myself." And he'd take care of Gemma as well.

No one would put any more bruises on Gemma Newhouse.

"Be careful," Rex warned.

Once Boone had let Rex out, he came back and checked on Gemma. Her cheeks were flushed, and she was warm now. He gave in to the urge to touch her and brushed her hair off her face. She had a bruise near her temple. Some asshole had probably hit her. His jaw tightened.

Being as careful as he could, he pulled her feet onto his lap. He cleaned her scratches and pressed some bandages over them. Next, he checked her legs and arms, then took care of her wrists.

He'd just finished up when she moved restlessly and made a small sound.

"Shh. You're safe now."

She made a scared noise, her eyelids still closed. She started fighting the blanket.

"Gemma." He touched her hand. "You're safe, I promise. I won't let anyone get to you."

Her head turned his way, but she was still asleep. Her fingers curled around his. Like his presence reassured her. She settled.

"I'll protect you." He touched her hair. It was so silky. She made a soft sound, and the blanket slipped, baring one full, perfect breast topped with a dusky-pink nipple.

Dammit. Boone hurriedly yanked the blanket up. He tried to ignore the image seared into his brain.

Shit. It'd been too long since he'd gotten laid. So long, he couldn't even remember the last time.

He sat back and stared at the ceiling. Gemma Newhouse was in danger, afraid, vulnerable. And the last time he'd checked, he wasn't an asshole. Or at least, not that big of an asshole.

Rising, he strode into the kitchen and drank a big glass of water. Atlas trotted in and sat, with what looked like an accusing gaze aimed Boone's way.

"Watch her." He slammed the glass down. "I have stuff to do."

He headed outside. His first stop was his woodpile. His hands curled around the worn wooden handle of his axe.

He'd found chopping wood to be the best activity to clear the shit out of his head. After splitting several logs, and working up a sweat, he started to feel a bit better. More in control.

His first order of business—keep Gemma safe. Rex was right. Whoever had orchestrated her abduction would be looking for her.

Why had they taken her? Was this about ransom? Something to do with her father?

Paul Newhouse owned a giant retail and tech company called Expanse. It was known for retail sales, but also did lots of behind-the-scenes technology for companies—servers, cloud computing, and other stuff he didn't fully understand. It wasn't his area of expertise. Boone was good with a gun and hand-to-hand combat, not computers.

What he'd told Rex rattled around in his head. He could definitely contact his old commander. A man Boone trusted with his life. If anyone could find out what was going on, it would be Vander Norcross.

There'd been no mention of Gemma's abduction in the news. That was weird. Why would her family not get a word out, to get people looking for her?

Right now, he had lots of questions and no answers.

He sliced the axe into a log, then left it. He scanned the growing darkness. Time for a quick perimeter check. His boots crunched on the twigs and dead leaves as he strode across the grass. He wanted to ensure that the high-tech sensors he had along the boundary were all in order.

He didn't want anyone sneaking up on him.

Boone also made a quick trip down to the riverbank to collect his fishing gear and his other pair of boots. On the way back, he studied his cabin. He suddenly wished he'd renovated the main house. It would be bigger, nicer for Gemma.

He shook his head.

She wouldn't be staying long. When she woke up, they'd talk and make a plan.

Before he knew it, Gemma Newhouse would be out of his life. Nothing but a distant memory.

MMM, there was nothing like being warm and cozy with morning light filtering into the room.

Except her comforter felt like wool and smelled like man.

Gemma blinked her eyes open and saw a whole lot of rustic cabin. She blinked again.

Her LA apartment was *not* rustic. The closest thing to rustic was the granite in her kitchen.

She sat up fast, then snatched the blanket closer. Oh God, she was naked.

What had happened? Her heart raced. She swallowed, her mouth so dry. Her head ached and her feet stung as well.

She scooched to the end of the couch. There was a side table with a hardback book and a glass of water resting on it. Some memories peppered her, making her heart race faster.

She'd been grabbed off the street in LA. Dragged into a van. *Abducted.*

Her breathing sped up, her hand twisted in the blanket. She was regretting telling her father she refused to have security dogging her every step. She'd had guards as a kid and she'd vowed to escape that once she became an adult.

But someone had drugged her, tied her up. It got blurry after that. She remembered traveling somewhere. The sound of being on a plane—that familiar drone.

Oh, hell. Where was she? Was she even in the USA anymore? Fear cramped her belly, and her fingers twisted in the blanket.

Then... Then... She pressed a palm to the side of her head. It hurt so much to think.

Wait. She'd been in a vehicle, and they'd pulled over and she'd escaped. She'd gotten her bindings loose and run. She'd run into trees and...

Ugh, why couldn't she remember?

She knew her name was Gemma Charlotte Newhouse. She lived in LA. She'd recently starred on the baking show *Cake and Bake.* She loved sugar. All kinds of sugar—brown, white, raw, powdered, caster. She knew she could make a mean chocolate cake, and a mouthwatering soufflé, and her macarons rocked. But the last twenty-four hours were a blurry, shadowy mess.

The door of the cabin opened.

She stiffened. The man was tall. His muscular frame

filled the doorway, and her heart kicked her ribs. The light behind him put his face in shadow.

A squeak escaped her, and fear exploded like a bag of dropped flour. She leaned over, grabbed the hardback off the table, and tossed it.

The man was fast. He dodged, and the book hit the floor.

"What the hell?" His voice was deep and smooth.

Gemma tucked her legs up, trying to get air into her lungs.

The man stepped forward, and now she saw his face. Bad guys shouldn't be so handsome.

He was frowning at her as a German Shepherd walked around him, then headed straight for Gemma.

She tensed, but the dog nudged her, looking friendly.

"Gemma, are you all right?"

Her gaze flew back to the man. Her brain registered that he didn't look threatening. And...his face was ruggedly handsome. There was nothing smooth about him, but he had a strong jaw combined with a long, muscled body. He was the kind of guy who'd be cast as the hero in an action movie.

"How do you know my name?"

The man's frown deepened. "You're sort of famous. And we met. Last night." He cocked his head. "You don't remember when I pulled you from the river?"

What? She licked her dry lips. Some flashbacks hit. Falling. Water. Cold.

Then a pair of worried, gold eyes.

She looked at those eyes now. "Boone?"

His frown eased. "That's right. My name's Boone Hendrix."

She tightened her hold on the blanket. "Did you take my clothes off, Boone?"

He stilled. A dull flush hit his cheeks. "Yes. You were wet and cold. I was concerned about hypothermia. I wrapped you in the blanket first. I didn't see a thing."

She shifted and saw the bandages on her sore feet. He'd taken care of her. Probably saved her life.

Most of her adult life, she'd learned to quickly assess people. To see if she could trust them. Were they after her dad's money? After an introduction to her father? Her high school boyfriend, who she'd had a huge crush on, who'd she'd trusted enough to give her virginity to, had just dated her to get access to her trust fund. It was an ugly memory she tried not to revisit. Unfortunately, she had a collection of them.

There were also people who didn't like her father, or disliked billionaires or what Expanse was doing, and believed they could hurt her to hurt him.

Yes, her radar for picking trustworthy people was pretty finely tuned. She didn't pick Boone Hendrix as a crazy rapist or abductor.

She cleared her throat. "Do you have something I could wear?"

"Sure. My stuff will likely be too big..."

"A T-shirt would be a good start."

"I hung your wet clothes in the bathroom." He gestured to a doorway on the other side of the room. "They should be dry later." He stalked through a different doorway, and came back with a folded, white T-shirt.

Clutching the blanket, Gemma headed for the bathroom. It was small and basic, but clean. She checked out the medicine cabinet. No drugs, just shaving gear all lined up with military precision. A light bulb went off. Military.

She'd bet her trust fund that Boone Hendrix had been in the military. She'd seen it in her father's security detail—the same bearing, the watchful gazes.

She found her underwear and tried not to be embarrassed that Boone had held them. Her bra and panties were still damp, as were her leggings and T-shirt.

Glancing in the mirror, she noted her hair was a tangled mess, and she had a bruise on her temple. She probed it gently. Then she dropped the blanket and checked her body.

Oh, man. She was covered in quite a few bruises and scratches. Her feet and calves were the worst. She rubbed her left hip and saw a nasty, inflamed scratch. The damn thing was itchy, which she hoped meant it was healing.

They'll all heal, Gemma. There was nothing life threatening.

She pulled Boone's T-shirt on. It swamped her, but was soft and freshly laundered. Man, it wasn't often she went without a bra. Her D cups needed support. But she'd have to make do.

She left the bathroom and found Boone pacing.

Another memory hit. "Wait? There was another man here."

Boone turned. "You said no to going to the hospital, but you'd lost consciousness. Rex is a friend." Boone cleared his throat. "He's the local vet."

"Vet?" A startled laugh slipped from her lips.

Boone's lips twitched. "Atlas can vouch for Rex. Although the man's bedside manner leaves a lot to be desired. He said you'd be fine. The drug was working its way out of your system. I cleaned the scratches on your feet."

Gemma pressed her palms to her cheeks. She felt everything cave in on her. "God. I was abducted, drugged. My family must be frantic."

Boone shoved his hands in his pockets. "There's been nothing in the news about you on the TV or the Internet."

She frowned. "Surely they'll contact my father for ransom."

"If this is about ransom."

A cold shiver hit her, then she remembered. "My parents are away. They aren't contactable."

Boone frowned. "I'm sure your father has a satellite phone."

"Oh, he owns a company that makes them, but they don't work at the bottom of the ocean."

Boone's eyebrows rose.

"My parents are in a deep-water submarine, in the Mariana Trench in the middle of the Pacific Ocean. It's a big trip for their anniversary. My father is a huge supporter of underwater research and marine conservation."

"Okay. Still, surely whoever took you would have issued their demands. Your father's security would have contacted the FBI."

But that hadn't happened. What the hell was going on? "What day is it?"

"Saturday."

She swallowed. "None of my friends would check on me. I took a week off work. I'm supposed to be at a yoga and culinary retreat in Big Sur."

"I'm guessing whoever took you timed it well."

God. "I'm afraid."

He took a step closer. "Don't be. You're not alone anymore. I'll help you."

"Why?" People always expected something. No one did anything for nothing. "You want to get a big paycheck?"

He made an angry noise. "No, because it's the right thing to do. The bastards who did this need to be stopped."

She blinked, warmth filling her chest. God, he really was a hero.

Maybe she could trust him?

"Boone, this will cause you problems. I should go."

He took another step closer. "Where?"

She wrung her hands together.

"How about we try to work out what's going on? Find out who's after you?"

She bit her lip. She didn't want to go. She didn't want to be alone.

He held out a hand. His palm was wide and calloused. Then Atlas nudged her leg.

"I'll contact a friend who can help," Boone added. "He can also vouch for me."

"Who is he?"

"He lives in San Francisco and owns a security company. Vander Norcross."

Her eyes widened. "You know Vander Norcross?" Vander had done work for her father.

Boone nodded.

Then Gemma dragged in a deep breath and put her hand in Boone's.

CHAPTER FOUR

Boone got the laptop set up just as Gemma strode back into the living area. He'd found her a pair of his shorts, and she'd folded the waistband over a few times.

His gaze dropped to her legs, then he looked away. He saw Atlas staring at him with an accusing look.

Damn judgmental dog.

Gemma sat down beside him. She looked much better after her shower. Her damp hair was in a braid, tied with a rubber band he'd found for her.

"Vander's company has done work for my father before." She tucked a loose strand of hair back behind her ear. "My dad says Vander is one man he'd never cross."

"We'll sort this out."

"Boone..." She pressed a hand to his knee. "Thanks for helping me."

"Anyone would."

"No, they wouldn't."

He frowned at her, sensing more to her words, but

the laptop screen flickered, and Vander Norcross appeared.

Boone's old commander was Italian-American, with dark hair, a serious face, and blue eyes so dark they looked black. He emitted that vibe that warned you not to mess with him. He had since the first day Boone had met him in Ghost Ops training.

"Boone," Vander said.

"Vander." The other man was used to being in charge, and he was damn good at it. Vander was a man who took action and got things done. A man who wasn't intimidated by anything.

Then Vander's dark gaze switched to Gemma. His expression didn't change, but Boone got the impression he was surprised. Although he'd never seen Vander surprised before.

"Gemma?"

She nodded. "Hi, Vander."

Frowning, Boone's old boss looked back at him. "Boone, why is Gemma Newhouse with you?"

"Because I fished her out of the river."

She made a sound and grabbed Boone's hand. "I was abducted."

Now Vander's face sharpened. He looked like a predator sensing blood in the water. "Tell me."

Gemma recounted her story, Boone filling in some of the gaps.

Vander sat back in his chair. "Gemma, I don't think your parents know. There hasn't been a whisper about this."

"They don't. No one knows this, but my parents are

doing a submarine trip to the Mariana Trench. They've been out of contact. It was top secret. You know how the shareholders get when Dad does anything the slightest bit risky."

Vander's frown deepened. "As far as we can tell, no one has reached out to your parents' people with a ransom demand."

"So, why did these men take me?" Her voice held the slightest wobble.

"Let me do some digging. Quietly." His dark gaze moved back to Boone. "You got this?"

Boone nodded. "Yes."

"Whoever took her is likely looking for her."

"I've got this."

Vander nodded. "I'll be in touch soon. Gemma, Boone is a good man. He's a hell of a soldier and you're in good hands. Boone, you keep her safe."

Boone closed the laptop. "You hungry? I'll make some breakfast."

She smiled. "I'm actually starving."

He froze. It was a beautiful smile that lit up her entire face.

"I'd sell my soul for a cup of coffee."

Boone shot to his feet. "Coffee and breakfast coming up."

And it was best if he put a little space between them.

Of course, she followed him into the kitchen.

His kitchen wasn't fancy, but it had always been enough for him. Right now, he wished he had some more kitchen...stuff. He put the coffee machine on.

"I'm not as good in the kitchen as you."

She hoisted herself up onto the scarred butcher-block counter. "I'm still learning. I mean, I've done some cooking courses." Her nose wrinkled. "Mom and Dad would have preferred that I used my degree, worked at Expanse, and had a stellar tech career. Or they would've been happy with a medical career, as well. My mom's a doctor."

Boone put some bacon in the frypan, then broke some eggs into a bowl and started mixing them. He figured he couldn't go wrong with scrambled eggs. "What's your degree?"

She pulled a face. "Computer science. I went to Stanford. It was during my 'try and please my parents' phase. I was good at it, but I never loved it. I'm pretty sure I was the only one in my coding class imagining making cupcakes."

"You like to bake. You're good at it."

Faint color filled her cheeks. "I don't hear that very often. Did Atlas tell you that?"

"Maybe I caught a bit of *Cake and Bake* while Atlas was watching."

That got him a smile, but then it dissolved. "Since *Cake and Bake* wrapped, I've just been working part time at a local bakery in LA." Her face lit up again. "The old Italian lady who runs it is an amazing baker. I've learned so much. And the rest of the time..."

Boone raised a brow. "The rest of the time?"

The pink in her cheeks darkened. "Um, I help out at a charity called Angel Cakes. We bake birthday cakes for kids in need. Kids who are sick, in foster homes, or kids from disadvantaged backgrounds where their parents might not be able to afford a cake."

The daughter of the richest man in America baked cakes for disadvantaged kids. She was absolutely nothing like he'd imagined her to be. He thought of the birthdays where he'd had no cake. His uncle had always taken him out for dinner and given him some money. But after he'd lost his parents, birthday cakes had been a thing of the past.

"That's really special, Gemma."

She smiled. "Thanks. I haven't even told my parents about Angel Cakes. My dad thinks all my baking is a waste of time. Mom thinks I'll grow out of this *phase*." She made air quotes as she said the word. "That I'm wasting my life on something so frivolous."

"Good food is not frivolous. As someone who's been forced to eat MREs in the field too many times to count, I really like good food. And I've learned that life's too short to do crap you don't want to do."

He thought of the friends he'd lost. The men who'd never see their kids grow up. Never live the life they'd imagined after the military. His throat tightened.

Gemma looked at the floor. "I wish my parents felt the same. They're always working, pushing for more." She sighed. "They think I'm wasting my potential."

"Is that why you went on *Cake and Bake*? To prove them wrong?"

"Maybe. To show that I had skills. That baking is a beautiful thing that can brighten someone's day, and that it matters." She sighed. "Not very useful when you've been abducted, though."

He tipped her chin up. "No one is getting their hands on you again."

More color filled her cheeks. "This is a lot of trouble for you—"

"No." He served up the eggs and bacon, then grabbed the toast that popped out of the toaster. He'd fight for her. It was who he was. A part of him hated seeing this nice, innocent woman upset, afraid, and anxious.

He set the food on his small table. He usually ate there alone. "For now, let's eat."

She nodded and hopped down. Atlas turned up, begging for snacks with his big brown eyes.

"Can I feed him?"

"Sure, but you'll never get rid of him ever again."

She gave Atlas some bacon. He eyed her adoringly.

Gemma only picked at her food. Boone noted that one of her legs was bouncing, and she was nibbling on her bottom lip.

"Gemma, you're safe."

Her gaze flicked up. "It's not easy to turn off the worry." She blew out a breath. "I'm sorry. It must be nothing compared to when you were deployed in dangerous countries. Facing deadly situations."

"Hey." He touched a hand. "This is a scary situation. I was trained and armed, and I had my team."

Meanwhile, assholes had attacked and drugged this woman, and she'd had no one.

She pushed to her feet and started pacing. Atlas watched her intently.

Boone watched the sunlight highlight her pretty face.

Her strides were jerky, and she clutched her hands in front of her.

"Gemma?"

She looked at him. "Sorry, I pace when I'm upset."

"What do you need to relax? To get your mind off things?"

"I need to bake."

"I DON'T HAVE much kitchen stuff."

Gemma waved a hand at Boone as she opened the cupboard doors and drawers. "I don't need fancy stuff."

She pulled out a chipped mixing bowl. She'd already found flour, sugar, milk, eggs, and a few other things she could use.

"I'm going to make cookies and a cake."

Atlas, who was sitting nearby, straightened. Gemma frowned at the dog.

"Not sure they're good for you, boy." She tapped a finger against her chin. "I need to do a little research on dog-friendly baking. Can I borrow your laptop?"

"Sure." Boone eyed his dog. "But a human-friendly cake is first priority."

She grinned at him. "Don't worry, big guy. Chocolate or vanilla?"

"Chocolate." His answer was instantaneous.

Her grin widened. Boone Hendrix liked chocolate. She felt a pop of warmth for his enthusiasm.

Her mom and dad never wanted to eat any cake, or

cookies, or pie. They were always on some healthy eating plan with their personal trainers.

"My grandmother used to bake. It's one of those clear memories, me as a little girl and her letting me stir the mixture in this giant bowl." Gemma started putting ingredients in the bowl in front of her. She cracked an egg. "Who made you chocolate cake when you were little?"

A strange look crossed his face. "No one."

She stilled. "No one?"

He looked away. "My parents died in a car accident when I was twelve. My uncle raised me. He wasn't much for baking."

Gemma's heart clenched. Her parents didn't understand her, often disappointed her, and they didn't hide that she disappointed them constantly. But they loved her in their own way. Her childhood had held plenty of good memories and privilege.

And her grandmother had been a soft, bright refuge from her workaholic parents.

She tried to picture a young Boone, which was kind of hard. It was tough to imagine him as anything other than tall with broad shoulders. But then her brain conjured up a tall, gangly boy. A young Boone raised by a bachelor uncle.

Had there been love in his house? Anything soft and sweet?

Well, today, she could give him soft and sweet.

"Prepare yourself for some chocolate cake."

Atlas made a whining sound.

"Right. And some awesome doggie treats. Let me get

this cake in the oven, and then I'll find some treat recipes to blow your doggie mind, Atlas."

Gemma finished mixing all the ingredients. The oven was old, but functional, and she found one pan she could use. It was the only pan.

"Boone, can you give me a hand?"

"Sure." He circled around behind her, and she handed him the bowl.

"Hold that, and tip it while I scrape the mixture into the pan."

He obediently tilted the bowl while she used a spoon to scrape the mixture out. But instead of scenting her mixed ingredients, she got a whiff of Boone—clean skin, soap, and an undertone of leather.

Her belly clenched. It was a totally normal reaction to a hot guy. It had been a long time since she'd been with a guy. Her last boyfriend had seemed nice until she realized that he'd been trying to get a job at her father's company.

Trust was not a commodity she had a lot of, lately. She scraped the bowl and moved the spoon too quickly. She splattered chocolate over both hers and Boone's hands.

"Oh, sorry."

Holding the bowl with one hand, he lifted his other hand and licked his fingers.

Her belly clenched even more. He had really nice hands, and a nice mouth.

"You shouldn't eat that," she said. "It has raw eggs in it."

He smiled. "I've eaten worse."

It was a hell of a smile. The flutters in her belly intensified. She imagined him licking other things. Like her.

Eek, Gemma. Stop fantasizing about the man.

"Right. Okay." She clumsily stepped back and hit the packet of flour with her elbow. It dropped to the floor, and a cloud of white puffed into the air.

"Oh, no!"

"Don't worry." Boone set the bowl down. They both moved toward the mess and collided. She pressed her hands to his shirt.

Gemma sucked in a breath. How could a man's chest be so hard?

They were both dusted in flour. He also had a streak of it on his face, caught in the scruff on his square jaw.

She'd also added two white handprints to his T-shirt.

"Sorry," she squeaked again.

He stepped closer. "You have flour in your hair."

She laughed. "Not the first time. Although it doesn't usually happen this dramatically." She stepped a little closer to his body.

Boone's head lowered. Her belly felt alive, and she went up on her toes.

Their lips were just an inch apart. Gemma's heart pounded. She'd never wanted anything as much as she wanted this man to kiss her.

Well, she was done waiting. She tilted her head and pressed her mouth to his.

Oh. Holy moly.

Her hands twisted in his shirt so she could pull him closer. His mouth was hot, his tongue stroking hers. He tasted like every delicious dessert she'd ever coveted.

He made a deep sound and angled his head to take the kiss deeper. *Yes.* That was exactly what she wanted. She wanted it faster, deeper, hotter.

She never wanted it to stop.

Suddenly, he stiffened, his hands gripping her biceps. "Crap, I'm sorry."

She frowned. "Why?"

"You've been through a lot. You're in a terrible situation. I know you're scared—"

"I'm not scared anymore. Thanks to you."

Something moved through his gold-brown eyes. "I'm no hero."

"I beg to differ." She slid her hands up his chest. "Boone?"

"Yeah?"

"I'm not scared, nor do I feel worried or pressured right now."

His brow creased. "Good."

"And I want you to kiss me again. Actually, I kissed you the first time. So, I want *you* to kiss *me* this time."

She felt his muscles tense. For a second, she was sure he was about to pull away.

Then he yanked her up and kissed her.

Oh. *Oh.*

Gemma threw her arms around his neck. Her body was flush against his. Then his tongue was in her mouth.

She moaned. The kiss turned hot, fast. It was even better than the first one. She needed this. Him.

Their tongues stroked, explored. He kissed her like the world was about to end, like he needed her. She plowed her fingers into his hair and pulled him closer.

It was just getting really good, when all of a sudden, he released her.

She felt dazed. She blinked and gripped the counter so she didn't topple over.

"I'm sorry," he gritted out.

Then he turned and stalked out like a predator was on his tail.

Gemma blinked again. *What just happened?*

She touched her lips. A kiss had never made her feel so lightheaded and giddy and...hungry.

She glanced at Atlas. "Well, your dad can kiss."

Atlas wagged his tail.

She blew out a breath. The only problem was the bit where he'd raced out like she had the plague. Oh, and the bit where he'd apologized for the best kiss ever.

There was a loud *thwack* from outside.

She walked to the window and nudged the curtain aside. Boone stood with an axe in his hand, chopping wood. She watched him swing the axe, muscles flexing.

Gemma moaned a little and pressed a palm to her belly. She was outrageously attracted to Boone Hendrix.

Most importantly, he made her feel safe in a way that she hadn't felt for a long time. She had no idea what to do with that.

Well, Boone liked to chop wood, but when things got stressful for her, she baked.

"Right, Atlas. Let's find some dog treats I can make for you."

CHAPTER FIVE

Tugging the blanket up, Boone turned on his side on the couch.

He muttered under his breath. The couch was perfectly fine for sitting on in front of a football game, but not designed for a six-foot, three-inch man to sleep on.

He turned onto his back and listened to the low crackle of the fire. He'd seen how much Gemma liked it, so he'd lit it again. The light flickered on the ceiling.

He thought of her lying in his bed. Only one room away.

"Shit," he murmured.

He knew she was just wearing one of his T-shirts, lying on his sheets, her thick, brown hair on his pillows.

With a groan, he threw an arm over his eyes. The memory of those kisses slammed into him.

Her warm, pliant mouth. Her taste. The sounds she'd made.

He blew out a breath and pulled the blanket over his bare chest. He was only wearing a pair of old sweatpants and he felt too damn hot. He drew in a deep breath and realized the cabin smelled like chocolate cake.

Every little thing made him think of Gemma.

Finally, sleep crept over him. As often happened, the nightmares crept in, too.

"Bogey on the roof. We're taking fire."

Julio's voice on the radio.

"I'm coming," Boone responded.

"There are too many." Miles sounded frantic.

"We're surrounded!" Charlie yelled.

The sounds of gunfire.

His team was under attack. His brothers.

"Hold on," Vander's cool voice. "We're incoming. We're two klicks out."

"Charlie is down!" Julio yelled. "Fuck."

A jumble of old images filtered through his brain. His racing heart as he ran into the village. Seeing the Taliban fighters attacking his friends.

Then a bullet winged his arm and he fell. A Taliban fighter stood over him, with a rifle aimed at his face.

It had only gotten worse from there. The four of them in a cage, stripped of their gear.

The group's leader standing at the bars, his eyes soulless. "You will tell me everything about your team, your mission, all military information." He looked at Miles. "Start with that one."

No. No.

Shouts echoed around Boone as they'd dragged Miles from the cell and strung him up. He felt helplessness choke him hard.

Why hadn't they taken him?

"No." Boone couldn't breathe. *Guilt tasted like dirt and ash.*

"Boone?"

His brows creased. It was a female voice.

"Boone, wake up." A cool hand touched his shoulder.

He jerked awake and heard a gasp.

It took his brain a second to process. He was in his cabin. On his couch. His hand was clamped on Gemma's delicate wrist.

He heard her swallow. "You were moaning. Having a nightmare."

He released her quickly. "Did I hurt you?"

"No."

He shifted, sat up, and scraped his hands over his face. "Sorry I woke you."

She was silent. Just a dark shadow in the room. Then she moved and sat down beside him.

"You get them a lot?"

His chest tightened. He didn't talk about it. Ever. "Not every night, but I get them. You woke me before the worst of it."

Because he knew from experience just how much worse it got.

"They're about when you were in the military?"

He stared straight ahead. This pretty woman with her smooth skin, curves, and delicate hands couldn't ever understand. Hell, he didn't want her to understand. "Yeah."

"You've...talked to someone?"

It felt like something squeezed his throat. "Yes. Had a

THE HERO SHE NEEDS

therapist when I got out." He'd talked until he couldn't talk anymore.

She leaned into the cushions. "What branch were you in?"

"I joined the Army. I ended up in Delta."

"Special forces. Wow." She paused. "You worked with Vander."

"He was my commander."

"That man is a whole lot of scary."

"He is. Makes him good in the field."

She tucked her legs up under her. "My father said Vander was in some special program. Ghost Ops." She paused. "You were, too?"

"I can't talk about it."

Ghost Ops took the best of the best from all the special forces to make elite teams. Teams that went to the worst places to do the worst, most impossible missions.

"You must've done some dangerous jobs."

His fingers curled into his palm.

"And seen some terrible things," she whispered quietly.

"I got out. I'm alive."

"But others didn't?"

"No, they didn't. Good men. With families."

"I bet their families are proud of them. Boone, thank you for your service. Because of men like you, and your friends, who fight for us, protect us, I've never seen terrible things."

The ever-present pressure inside him eased just a little. It was why he'd served. He was good at it, but he believed in protecting his country. Protecting innocents from the bad in the world.

"Thanks, Gemma."

She nudged him. Her warm body was so close to his.

Lock it down, Hendrix.

"So, what else do you and Atlas watch on TV? Apart from *Cake and Bake*?"

"Football."

"Mm. What's your favorite team?"

"The Packers."

"I'm a Broncos girl, myself."

"Not the Rams?"

As they talked, he eased into the cushions, his body relaxing. The last grip of the nightmare leaked away. He liked her voice. It had a low, sexy undertone to it.

Somehow talk of football turned to favorite foods, favorite movies, then Boone sharing about living in small town Vermont.

But before he knew it, Gemma was leaning into his side, tucked up against him. He felt her shiver and wrapped his arm around her. He pulled the blanket over both of them.

They kept talking. And for Boone, the world just disappeared.

In that quiet moment in front of the fireplace, there was no bad stuff in the world, no wars, no old scars, and no nightmares.

BOONE WOKE to a warm weight resting on top of him.

He frowned, and realized he was lying on his back on the couch, with Gemma lying on top of him.

Damn. She was warm, her face in profile where it rested against his chest. She looked relaxed. She had really long eyelashes.

His cock responded to the feel of her, lengthening.

Shit.

He liked this. Liked her. Too much. Gemma Newhouse was not for him.

He was just keeping her safe. That was it.

Slowly, he shifted, and she made a cute, sleepy sound, and rubbed her cheek on his bare pec. His cock got harder.

Closing his eyes, he moved a hand to nudge her off him...and touched skin.

Oh, hell. He slid his hand over her. He realized her shirt had ridden up, baring her ass.

She wasn't wearing any panties.

His fingers tightened on lush skin. He froze and counted to ten. He opened his eyes...and saw his dog glaring at him accusingly from beside the couch.

Jesus. Cursing in his head, Boone maneuvered. He slid Gemma onto the couch and stood.

She turned, snuggling into the cushions. He hesitated, then tucked the blanket around her.

He turned and shot his dog a look. "What are you looking at?"

Atlas gave a low woof.

Jaw tight, Boone headed for the front door. He flexed his fingers.

He really needed a distraction.

STRETCHING, Gemma opened her eyes and smiled.

She felt well rested and relaxed.

Warm, aged, golden wood came into view. *Oh.* Boone's cabin. Everything rushed in on her.

The abduction. The men after her.

Ugh. Suddenly, she didn't feel so great.

Although, the memories of being held tight in Boone's arms as they'd slept on the couch were good.

She sat up. There was no sign of him, even though it was still early.

She rose and pushed her tangled hair back. She could hear a rhythmic *thwack, thwack, thwack* that she now recognized.

Peering out of the window, she spotted Boone at the woodpile. She almost swallowed her tongue. He was shirtless, with just gray sweatpants riding low on his lean hips.

Holy moly. She felt like a sugar rush had just hit. He was ripped. He had hard muscles and delineated ridges at his abdomen. She'd seen plenty of in-shape guys in California, but she knew for Boone, these muscles were hard earned. They were ones he used in real life, not just in the gym.

He'd clearly been at it for a while. His skin was sheened with sweat.

He looked like he was working off his demons. She remembered a few of the things he'd shared the night before.

She knew that it must just be the tip of the iceberg.

Whatever he'd seen and done and endured, even if it was for the greater good, had left scars.

She wanted to do something nice for him.

In the kitchen, she hummed to herself as she made some hot chocolate. She found two stainless-steel travel mugs and poured the drinks. It was her own special, ultra-chocolatey recipe.

She wrapped the blanket around her shoulders and slipped her feet into a pair of Boone's boots at the door. They were huge, and she knew she must look ridiculous.

But abducted women pulled from rivers couldn't be choosy.

Holding the two mugs, she nudged the door open, then headed in Boone's direction. The air was crisp and fresh. So different from California.

His back was to her, all those muscles flexing. The light flutters in her belly turned to liquid warmth.

She'd seen videos on social media like this—hot mountain men chopping wood. At the time, she hadn't entirely understood the appeal.

She bit her lip. Now she did. She spotted Atlas in the distance, sniffing around some trees. Boone sensed her and slammed the axe into the wood. He turned his head in her direction.

Now the liquid heat inside her spread everywhere. His gaze drifted down her body, then jerked back to her face.

"Morning." She held out one mug. "Hot chocolate. My own secret recipe."

"Thanks." He took it.

She tried not to notice when his fingers brushed hers.

But the tingles were outrageous. She watched him take a sip of his drink.

"It's good," he said.

She smiled at him, then sipped her own. She made a hum of pleasure.

When she looked up, Boone was looking at her mouth. Then he looked away, staring at Atlas. "I'm sorry I woke you last night."

She took a deep breath. "I'm not."

His head turned. His eyes looked like molten gold today.

Gemma shrugged a shoulder. "It's the best sleep I've had in a long time. And I don't just mean since I was taken." She looked at the trees, the beautiful riot of colors. "Thanks to my father's success, I find it hard to trust. And I often feel like a target." She met Boone's gaze. "You don't make me feel like that." She quickly sipped again. "I'm sorry for what you went through when you were deployed. It makes me realize that my problems pale a lot in comparison."

"You can't compare. Everyone has something to deal with."

"True. And Boone, I don't want apologies for the kisses, either. They were the best kisses of my life."

His face turned unreadable.

She'd said her piece. She'd leave him to chew on it. Turning, she wandered toward the old farmhouse. It was rundown, with its white paint faded and peeling, and several windows boarded up. But she could see the charm, with its classic peaked roof and large porch. She'd put a swing on it so she could sit and look at the trees while she sipped her hot chocolate.

There was a red barn not far from it, which looked like it was in good repair. She guessed the barn was of more use to Boone than a large farmhouse.

Atlas bounded her way, and she smiled.

"My uncle said the farmhouse needed too much work. And was too big for him."

Boone's voice came from right behind her.

"Makes sense. It looks like it needs a family." She walked up the sagging porch steps and looked in one grimy window. *Oh.* She saw a kitchen with an old-fashioned stove and a large farmhouse sink. The room was filled with dust, but light poured into the space. With some love and attention, and probably a big budget, it could be stunning.

She turned.

Boone stood with one boot resting on a step, an unbuttoned flannel shirt now on his body, and he was coiling some rope between his hands.

She stared at the rope and a sudden memory cut across her consciousness.

Rough hands tying her up. A wave of nausea. Feeling the prick of a needle at the back of her neck.

Her mug fell from nerveless fingers. It hit the porch, hot chocolate spilling.

"Newhouse won't be able to stop us."

"Yes. She'll give us exactly what the boss wants."

"I hope she fights. I hope we get to hurt her."

Fear was like a deluge—cold and paralyzing. It left her heart racing.

"Gemma. Gemma!"

Strong hands gripped her arms. Her skin felt so cold.

"Gemma?"

She looked up into Boone's face.

"You're safe." He cupped her cheeks. "Look at me."

She focused on him. He had a small scar on one eyebrow, and she wondered how he'd gotten it.

"That's it," he said slowly. "You're here with me."

"I remembered something. There were four men." She shivered. "They wanted to use me for something. They said my father couldn't stop them."

"Were they after money? Ransom?"

She shook her head. "No. It wasn't clear, but they didn't mention money. It felt like something else."

"Okay, that's good."

"They had a syringe. They held me down. One said he wanted to hurt me—" Her voice broke.

"You're safe, Gemma." He pulled her into his arms. "I'm not letting *anyone* get you."

She clung to him and absorbed his strength. A horrible thought hit her—what if Boone got hurt protecting her? What if those men hurt him, or worse?

Anger hit her hard.

She wrenched away. "How dare they? How dare they do this? Come after me, force my dad to do who knows what? Who does that?" She threw her arms in the air.

Atlas appeared, watching her carefully. He brushed against her leg.

"Those damn assholes are scum!" She whirled and stomped down the steps. "I was minding my own business when they snatched me off the street. They're, they're..." She ran out of steam.

"You done?" Boone asked, looking like he was fighting a smile.

She patted Atlas. "I guess. I could rant a bit more."

"Make you feel better?"

She sniffed. "Maybe."

"Then rant away."

She smiled.

"How about we make more hot chocolate? The stuff was good, and you didn't get to drink yours." He walked to her and tucked the blanket securely around her shoulders.

She nodded. "All right. I never say no to chocolate."

CHAPTER SIX

"We have some news."

Boone nodded at the laptop. Vander was on the screen.

Beside Boone, Gemma shifted on the couch, tucking her legs underneath her.

After her freakout earlier, she seemed okay. She'd spent some time drinking her hot chocolate and throwing a ball with Atlas. After that, she'd found a book to read in the loft.

But Boone could still see the strain she was under. The tense way she held herself, and the lines bracketing her mouth.

"You know who abducted me?" she asked.

"Not exactly. I'll let my tech guy explain." The image zoomed out. There was another man sitting beside Vander.

He had bronze skin and long hair pulled back in a stubby ponytail. "Hi, Gemma, I'm Ace."

"Nice to meet you."

"Sorry for what's happened to you."

"Thanks." She fiddled with the end of her braid.

"I've analyzed any CCTV cameras within a fifty-mile radius of Boone's farm." Ace made a face. "There aren't many up that way in the boonies."

"We like it like that," Boone said.

Ace gave an exaggerated shudder. "Anyway, I didn't expect to find anything. But I got lucky."

An image appeared. It showed a big, black SUV on an empty road.

"This is a camera set up to monitor wildlife crossing roads," Ace told them.

Gemma leaned forward. "That's the vehicle I was in!"

Ace tapped the keyboard. The image zoomed in and showed a view of the faces of the driver and passenger.

Both tough-looking, unsmiling men.

"I can tell there are two more in the back, but the windows are tinted too dark to get a good view of them," Ace added.

"Gemma, do you recognize them?" Vander asked.

She bit her lip. "Maybe? I'm not sure." She nervously rubbed her still-red wrists.

Boone reached out and grabbed her hand. Their fingers tangled, and she held on tight.

"My memories are still hazy," she said.

"It's fine," Boone said.

She looked back at the screen. "Who are they?"

"Romanians. Radu and Nicolescu. Both ex-military. Mercenaries for hire."

"Someone hired them to snatch Gemma," Boone said.

"Yes." Vander gave a curt nod. "It's that someone we haven't identified yet."

Boone bit back a curse. "Do you know where Radu and Nicolescu are now?"

"No sign of them. But they're pros. They won't have given up."

Gemma made a sound, and Boone squeezed her fingers.

"Gemma, don't leave Boone's side. I promise we're working behind the scenes. We are going to sort this out."

"Any word from my parents?"

Vander shook his head. "I spoke with their head of security. The dive will be over soon. We should be able to reach them then."

"Thank you." Her voice was shaky.

Boone hated seeing her so scared. "Talk soon, Vander." Boone lifted his chin, then closed the laptop.

That's when Atlas tried to get into Gemma's lap.

She gave a shaky laugh. "You're too big, Atlas."

Boone smiled. His dog was trying to cheer her up.

"How about an early dinner?" he suggested. "I have some steaks."

She gave him a small smile. "Sure."

But through the simple meal, she was quiet and subdued. They ended the evening in front of the fire, with Gemma drinking more of her delicious hot chocolate, Boone eating a huge slice of chocolate cake, and Atlas munching on the dog biscuits Gemma had made especially for him.

"What are your plans?" He glanced her way. "After this is over? You going to keep working at that bakery?"

"I'm not sure. I still have a few interviews to give, thanks to *Cake and Bake*. I'm evaluating my options." She sighed, staring at the fire. "I'm dragging my feet. I guess I don't want to live with my parents' constant disapproval."

"They love you?"

"Yes, in their own way. They're driven, but they aren't monsters."

"Then they'll want you to be happy."

"I wish it was that simple. I envy you having no parental pressure." She straightened, her face stricken. "I didn't mean that the way it sounded—"

"I know."

"I wish you'd never lost your parents, Boone. It must've been horrible. I hope your uncle was good to you."

"As good as a crusty old bachelor could be. He was my dad's brother. Older." Boone set his mug down. "But one thing he always did was support me, whatever I wanted to do. Gemma, it's your life. What do you want to do?"

White teeth worried her plump bottom lip. Lips he'd kissed.

"I had friends who never got to do all the things they'd dreamed about after the military. Don't think, just tell me."

"I want to open a bakery. Nothing fancy, just a simple place that uses good ingredients. I want to know the regulars who come in for their favorite things."

Boone nodded. "There you go."

"Starting a business is a big risk. Most fail, and while it isn't the financial part that would affect me, obviously, I couldn't stand for it to flop. To have my parents say they'd warned me. And there would be press." Her voice deepened. "Billionaire's daughter fails to get business to thrive."

"Most things worth having require some risk. And I reckon you have an expert who'd be happy to share his knowledge, help you mitigate some of those risks."

Her shoulders sagged. "He'd try to take over. He'd start talking about expanding into dozens of locations. Dad can't do small." She yawned, slapping a hand over her mouth.

"You're tired. Why don't you head to bed and get some sleep?"

"Boone, I can sleep on the couch. I hate that I've kicked you out of your own bed."

"The couch is comfy."

"I know."

Their gazes met. Oh, it'd been far too good waking up with her in his arms on the couch.

She shot to her feet. "Right, okay, sleep well."

"I will, Gemma." She hurried into the bedroom, and Atlas rose and followed her.

Boone rolled his eyes. "You are so easy."

And here he was, jealous of his own dog.

———

A HAND PRESSED over Gemma's mouth, wrenching her from a deep sleep.

Terror was an instant punch to her system.

She flailed. *Oh, God.* They'd found her. What had they done to Boone?

"Shh, it's me." Boone's low voice. "Sorry. You need to be quiet."

Gemma sagged with relief. He was a dark shadow beside the bed.

"Someone tripped my exterior sensors."

She pushed his hand down. "What?"

"We have company."

Her heart rabbited. *Oh, shit.*

"Get dressed. We need to move."

Her eyes adjusted enough to see that he was already dressed.

"Gemma, hurry."

She nodded and shoved the sheets off.

"No lights," he warned.

She scrambled around the room and pulled on her now clean and dry leggings, a T-shirt of Boone's, and one of his sweaters. It swamped her, but it would have to do. She pulled her hair up in a quick messy bun. Next, she pulled on a pair of Boone's socks.

"Here." He reappeared. "I have some running shoes that were too small for me."

"They'll do." She'd need a second pair of socks, but they'd do.

Boone moved toward a window.

"Can you see them?"

"I've flagged two bogeys coming up the driveway. They're sticking to the shadows."

Her chest locked. They were here for her.

"I assume the other two we clocked from the SUV are here as well." She saw him open a cabinet. Atlas was silent, alert. The glow from the fireplace gave enough light to illuminate the huge rifle and handguns Boone pulled out.

Her stomach clenched. "Boone..."

He swiveled, crossed to her and cupped her jaw. "It's going to be all right."

"I don't think it is."

"Here's the plan. We're leaving. You're going to follow me to the barn, where I have another truck. We'll be gone before they have a chance to follow."

Her throat was impossibly tight. "I don't want you to get hurt."

There was a flash of his white teeth in the darkness. "You don't need to worry about me."

But she would. He was a good man, putting himself in the line of fire for her.

"Ready?" he asked.

She wasn't going to cause him more trouble or get in his way. "Ready."

"Good. We'll go out the window at the side of the cabin. They'll be watching the doors. Stick close to me, and we'll move through the shadows. Stay low."

She nodded. Her heart was pounding so hard in her chest that it hurt.

They moved into a tiny laundry room. Boone opened the window, and she watched him snap his fingers at Atlas. The dog leaped out.

Boone threw a leg over the windowsill and followed, looking smooth and stealthy.

"Come on," he whispered.

She swung her leg over and was not so graceful. She half tumbled out the window into Boone's arms. He set her on her feet.

He lifted a hand and made a signal that she guessed meant to follow him. She stayed right behind his broad back. They set off across the grass, staying as close to the trees as they could. Ahead, the large shadow of the barn loomed in the distance.

She was tempted to look around, but she just focused on keeping up with Boone.

With every step, she expected to hear a shout, or a gunshot.

She was relieved when they finally reached the barn. Boone pressed his back to the wood and pulled her close. Atlas stayed nearby.

Boone tugged her toward the doorway. It was pitch black inside the structure.

"Wait in here with Atlas." His mouth brushed her ear, and he nudged her against the wall, just inside the barn. "I need to get some things. Stay hidden."

"Okay."

She hated to admit it, but she was scared to be left alone. She swallowed hard as Boone disappeared into the darkness.

Gemma dragged in a breath. Then Atlas brushed her leg, and she ran a hand over his fur.

Knowing the dog was with her helped.

Again, anger that this was happening filled her. She felt like a hunted animal. She scrubbed a hand over her face.

Then Atlas stiffened. He was staring at the large door into the barn.

Fear clogged her throat. She couldn't see anything. Her pulse drummed. She shifted against the wall, trying to stay deep in the shadows.

Suddenly, a dark shadow charged through the door, right at her.

Gemma grunted as the man hit her, and they slammed into the wall.

"Should have stayed still, then I might not have seen you." The man gripped her throat. "You've caused us a lot of trouble, bitch."

It was the man who'd said he wanted to hurt her. She recognized his accented voice. Without stopping to think, Gemma rammed her palm into his nose.

He growled, and she twisted to escape. He grabbed her hair and pulled.

No. The pain in her scalp brought tears to her eyes. This wasn't happening.

"Keep fighting, girl," he said. "Give me an excuse to hurt you."

"*Asshole,*" she bit out.

He grabbed the front of her sweater and pulled her up on her toes.

There was a low, dangerous snarl, right before Atlas slammed into the man.

"What the fuck?"

He went down with the large German Shepherd on top of him. The man yelled.

Gemma couldn't see what Atlas was doing, but the man's screams intensified.

"Gemma." Boone reappeared. "Okay?"

"Yes," she replied shakily. "One mercenary found me."

"Let's go. Atlas."

The dog released her attacker. Boone leaned over the man and punched him. The man didn't get up. Boone pulled her deeper into the dark barn. A second later, she saw the silhouette of a truck.

He opened the passenger door. "In."

She climbed in, shivering as the adrenaline rush hit.

Atlas bounded in behind her. Boone circled the truck and got into the driver's seat. He started the engine.

"Buckle up." Then he stepped on the accelerator.

They sped out of the barn. She got a brief glimpse of some men running toward them.

Then she heard gunshots.

Oh, God.

"Down." Boone pushed her head down.

The truck fishtailed in the gravel, then picked up speed.

A moment later, they were on the road.

"We're fine." Boone checked the mirrors. "They're not following. Or if they are, they're too far behind."

She sat up, trying to stop her shaking.

"You're safe." His shadowed face was set in hard lines.

She nodded.

Then Atlas leaned into her, sharing his warmth.

"Thank you." She held on tight. "Both of you."

She was safe for now. But how long would that last?

CHAPTER SEVEN

The headlights cut through the darkness. Boone's hands clenched hard on the wheel.

Gemma was quiet beside him, but not asleep. He felt her tension. They'd been driving for an hour, and he'd spent most of it checking for a tail. He'd taken a circuitous route through the back roads to avoid detection. Luckily, he knew them like the back of his hand.

He turned off the main road and headed down a narrow dirt track. The truck bumped along the uneven ground.

Gemma stirred. "Where are we?"

"We need to change vehicles. They saw this one. They have the resources to track it." He pulled up beside a dilapidated barn.

"Whose place is this?"

"A friend of my uncle. His house is a few miles away." Boone grabbed his flashlight from the glove compartment, then climbed out and headed for the barn door. It needed a lot of force to open it.

He clicked on his flashlight. His uncle's old Ford truck was parked inside, the red paint coated in a thick layer of dust.

But Boone kept it fueled and roadworthy. Along with a stash of clothes and weapons.

Atlas sniffed around. Gemma looked hesitant and wrapped her arms around herself.

His jaw clenched. She'd been through so much. "You holding up okay?"

She looked up. "No. But I'll be okay. I refuse to let these people destroy my life. I have no idea what they want, but it'll be the same as everyone else who's targeted me in the past. Money and power."

His brow creased. "This has happened before?"

She shrugged a shoulder. "There were a couple of kidnapping threats when I was younger. One attempt. The worst isn't the overt bad guys. It's the people who befriend you, act like they like you, when really, they just wanted access to my father."

"I'm going to get you safe." He cupped his hands over her shoulders. "I don't care about your father."

"It's not your job, Boone."

"It is now."

Their gazes locked.

"And just for the record," he said. "I see you. Not your father's money or influence. You."

She made a sound. He pulled her close and hugged her hard. She held on tight.

"What happens now?" she asked.

"I'm going to message Vander with an update. Then we go dark."

Her head jerked. "Go dark?"

"We have no idea how they found you at my place. My guess, they've been checking out properties along the river. But it's best to ditch my phone, just in case, and I'll pick up a burner."

She blew out a breath. "Okay. Then?"

"Road trip."

"To where?"

"Away from here. I have buddies from my Ghost Ops team scattered around the country. They'll help."

"So, you know a whole bunch of heroes?"

"Just men who want to do the right thing." His chest tightened. Mainly because they'd seen the wrong thing too many times. Been forced to do lots of wrong things in the name of the right thing.

He pulled out his phone, messaged Vander, then turned his phone off. He stashed it on the dusty workbench.

"We'll get on the road, and then you try to get some sleep."

He opened the tailgate on the Ford and climbed up. He opened a storage box on the back. He had clothes and gear wrapped in plastic. He pulled out a blanket and handed it to her.

She gave him a small smile.

"Atlas, quit exploring." Boone gave a whistle. "Time to go."

The dog bounded over and jumped into the cab.

Once they were all settled, Boone started the engine. It ran with a well-tuned purr. He reversed out, then pulled his truck in, and closed the barn up. He kicked leaves over the tire tracks.

Soon, they were out on the road, their headlights illuminating the trees.

"They won't stop, will they?" she said quietly.

"They're pros, Gemma. Their reputation depends on them finishing a job."

"God."

He reached out over the top of a snoozing Atlas and touched her arm. "I'm not letting them get one finger on you."

She nodded and let out a large exhale. "So, where exactly are we going?"

"Colorado."

"Colorado! That's like two thousand miles away."

"Right. The last place these mercenaries will expect you to be."

"One of your buddies lives there?"

"Yep. Shep isn't fond of people. He has a cabin in the Rocky Mountains."

"Ah. That sounds familiar. Is that a requirement for your friends?"

"What?"

"A loner personality with a cabin in the woods?"

He laughed, then quiet for a moment. "We carried out classified missions."

She was quiet for a moment. "Hard missions."

His hands flexed on the wheel. "Yeah. We didn't come back whole. Being part of regular society isn't easy."

"So it's easier to be alone."

He stared through the windshield. He saw the faces of his lost brothers. "Yeah. Get some sleep now, Gemma."

"All right."

She shifted around and settled with her head against the window. Atlas leaned into her.

Finally, she went still. Her quiet breathing was the only sound in the cab.

She was holding up well. He hadn't expected a billionaire's daughter to have steel under her smooth skin and freckles.

GEMMA WOKE with an ache in her neck, and her hip itching like crazy. Scratching her hip, she felt the healing cut marring her skin. She straightened, then stared through the windshield at the open road and remembered everything.

The sun was shining, and the truck was filled with the drone of the wheels on the road. They were heading down some highway. Atlas had his head in her lap.

She looked at Boone. He drove well—steady and in control. Her gaze fell on his strong hands. Hands that had protected her.

He didn't look tired, even though he must've been driving for hours.

"Hey," he said.

"Hi." Atlas moved his head, and she rubbed between his ears. "Where are we?"

"Ohio."

"You must be exhausted."

"Not really. I've had to stay up for far longer than this, and in much worse conditions."

Gemma felt a catch in her belly. She couldn't even imagine how tough he was, what he'd endured.

"Hungry?" he asked. "I figured we'd find a place for some breakfast."

Her stomach rumbled at the thought of food. "Is it safe to stop?"

"I think so. I'll head off the highway for a bit to make sure. I had a stash of cash in my gear, so we won't use a credit card."

She plucked at the oversized sweater she wore. "My outfit is really good for dining in."

He glanced at her. "You look fine. We'll pick up some clothes for you when we can. My stash only has stuff in my size."

Boone pulled off the highway. They ended up in a small, out-of-the-way town. He pulled up in front of a diner.

"Atlas, stay in the truck." Boone cracked the window. "I'll bring you back breakfast."

The dog gave a low woof.

They entered the diner. It was like stepping back in time. Wooden tables and booths, scarred linoleum floor, some kitschy clocks on the walls.

"Hi, there." A smiling older lady intercepted them. "Take a seat. The menus are on the table. I'll be back to take your order soon."

Gemma went to sit in a booth near the door, but Boone grabbed her hand. He pulled her to another booth. "Sit beside me, on this side."

She realized how alert he was, scanning the other occupants of the diner.

Nodding, she slid into the seat, and he followed her in. His thigh brushed hers and she felt a flush of warmth.

"Why this table?" she whispered.

"Safer. No entry or exit behind us. I can see everyone who enters from here."

Did he ever shut off that constant vigilance? Did he ever relax?

Boone perused the menu. Gemma did as well and decided to keep it simple.

The waitress pulled out a notepad. "Right, what will it be?"

"The big breakfast for me," Boone said. "Extra serving of bacon, please. And coffee, black."

"Gotcha, handsome. And for your beautiful wife?"

Gemma blinked and glanced at Boone. He slid an arm around her. "Honey?"

Her pulse did a little skitter. "Scrambled eggs on toast, please. And orange juice and a cappuccino."

"I'm on it."

"So, we're married now?" Gemma asked softly, after the waitress had gone.

"Doesn't hurt. If the mercs track us, they're looking for a single man and woman, not a married couple. Muddies the trail a little bit." He looked out the window. "I see a pay phone. I want to call Vander. Anyone bothers you, come to me."

She nodded.

She watched him walk away with that athletic stride

of his. A man who could handle whatever life threw at him.

Boone Hendrix had already proven that.

"Darlin', I don't blame you for eyeing your man like that." The waitress set their drinks down. "That man is a prime American hunk." She made a humming noise.

Heat filled Gemma's cheeks. "Ah, thanks."

The older woman leaned in, a conspiratorial look on her face. "Tell me he can kiss like a dream, too."

Gemma didn't need to lie. "He can."

The waitress pressed a hand to her heart. "Hold on to him tightly, sweetheart. They don't make many like him anymore. I do say, he looks like a man who carries some baggage, too, though. He a cop?"

"He was in the military."

"Ah." The woman nodded. "When things get hot, you hold on tight. Something tells me your man needs some sweet and soft, as well as some strength. I think you've got all of that. I'll get your food."

Gemma was eating some very good eggs when Boone returned. He pulled his plate in a little bit closer.

"Vander's up to speed. He said to lay low. And he spoke with your father."

"He's okay?" She straightened. "And my mom?"

Boone nodded. "Their security team has been briefed, and your parents are on their way to LA. They're worried about you."

She felt a wave of love. Their relationship wasn't perfect, but they were hers, and they loved her.

"Eat up. Atlas will be desperate for his bacon soon.

There's a Walmart one town over. We'll get some clothes for you there."

They ate their breakfast, and Boone paid the bill. The waitress gave Gemma a wave and a wink as they left.

As predicted, Atlas was wiggling with excitement, ready to eat his bacon. The dog wolfed it down quickly.

Soon, they were back on the road.

"It's my turn to pick the tunes next," she said.

His lips quirked. "We're taking it in turns? I thought the driver got to pick."

"I'm your wife. It's your job to make me happy."

He shot her a look that made her skin tingle.

"I'll do my best."

CHAPTER EIGHT

W hen Boone pulled into the Shady Rest Inn just outside of Springfield, Illinois, he caught the look on Gemma's face.

"It's not that bad."

She shot him a look. "Shady is the right adjective."

"I know, but the mercs will search the good hotels looking for you. No one will expect Paul Newhouse's daughter to stay here."

"Boone, no one would expect anyone's daughter to stay here."

He cut the engine. "It's dog friendly."

She made an unconvinced noise. "Pretty sure Atlas doesn't want to stay here, either."

"Come on. We both need some rest." He reached for the box of pizza that they'd just picked up for dinner. "Stay in the truck, so the receptionist only sees me." He handed her the box.

She nodded.

As he walked into reception, he kept an eye on her as

he showed his fake ID and paid the bored-looking lady at reception with cash. The woman was more interested in watching her television show on a small TV.

He walked back to the truck and helped Gemma out. He grabbed their bags, and they made their way to their room. The paint on the building had once been white, but it had faded to a pale, stained beige. The trim was a chipped green.

Gemma was now wearing jeans that fit her perfectly and a new sweater from Walmart. And some running shoes in her own size. She looked like a college student.

He unlocked the door and frowned. The lock was barely worth the effort. The room had two double beds, stained carpeting, and the vague smell of old cigarette smoke.

"I take it back," Gemma said. "This place is five stars. Nothing beats stale cigarette smoke oozing from dirty carpet."

Ignoring the sarcasm, he nudged her inside. "It'll smell like pizza soon enough."

Boone fed Atlas while Gemma sat cross-legged on one bed and bit into a slice of pizza. He took a chair at the rickety table.

"I used to dream of taking a road trip when I was younger. Just getting in my car and driving away. Go and live a normal life." She looked around. "This isn't exactly what I had in mind."

Boone snorted.

"I've been thinking about my abduction," she said.

He lowered his slice of pizza. "And?"

"I don't think it's about money."

"What makes you say that?"

"They haven't given up. They *really* want something." Her brow wrinkled.

"Did you hear something they said? About exactly what they were after or who they work for?"

"I don't know. It's all still blurry." She bit into a second slice of pizza, chewed, and then swallowed. "There are still things I can't remember."

"You know much about your father's company?"

"No. I'm a baker, remember."

"But you worked for him for a few years."

"Yes." She licked her fingers. "After I graduated from college, I worked at Expanse." She blew out a breath. "I was miserable. Every day my soul died a little."

"I think it's brave that you finally did what you really wanted to do."

She smiled. "Thanks."

"So, you know some of your dad's business."

"Sure. Some of the behind-the-scenes stuff with the systems. I worked on a few different projects." She shook her head. "Nothing that seems worthy of being abducted." She frowned.

"What is it?"

She rubbed her forehead. "I feel like there's a memory right there. I can't quite see it clearly." She blew out a frustrated breath.

"Don't try to force it. It'll come in time."

"I hope so. I want to stop these guys and get my life back."

"You'll get there."

She rose. "I think I'll take a shower." She grabbed

some of her new clothes from the plastic bags and entered the tiny bathroom.

That's when it hit Boone. She was right there, behind that door, undressing.

He dragged in a breath and reached for the bottle of water he'd gotten at the pizza place. He wished it was a beer.

Atlas was watching him.

"Why aren't you sleeping, huh?" Boone made himself eat another slice of pizza as he heard the water in the shower turn on. He wondered where else Gemma Newhouse had freckles on her skin.

"Get a grip, Hendrix," he muttered.

Just as he finished the pizza, the shower cut off.

Then, Gemma screamed.

His instincts fired, and he snatched up his Glock. He crossed the room in two strides and shoved open the bathroom door.

She was standing on a threadbare mat, skin and hair damp, wrapped in a skimpy white towel. She gasped.

He scanned the small room for the threat.

There was no one there.

"What's wrong?"

"There was a cockroach."

He drew in a breath. "A cockroach."

"It was the size of a small pony, Boone." She shifted and slipped a little on the mat. She lost her grip on one side of her towel. It slipped, baring one high, full breast, and one side of her body.

Boone couldn't look away, and he watched her nipple bead under his gaze.

Fuck. His cock swelled.

Then Atlas butted into the room, knocking Boone forward a step. Instinctively, he gripped Gemma's hip. The bare one. She gasped again.

Atlas barked, looking for a threat, as well. There wasn't enough room for the three of them.

"Atlas, out," Boone said.

The dog whirled and hit the back of Gemma's legs. She pitched forward into Boone's chest. He went back a step and sat down on the closed toilet seat lid.

Gemma landed on top of him, straddling him.

His dog headed out, just as Gemma lost her grip on her towel.

It slipped to the floor.

Boone found himself eye level with both her bare breasts now. Blindly, he set the Glock on the sink.

Gemma gripped his shoulders, her chest rising and falling. Her nipples were tight buds.

He couldn't move, except to swallow. "I know I should get up and leave."

"So why don't you?" she whispered.

"Because I really fucking want to suck one of your pretty nipples into my mouth."

Her breath hitched. "So why don't you?"

DESIRE FELT like fireworks inside her. Gemma's belly was alive with hot flutters.

The way Boone was looking at her...

She trembled. He did nothing more than just stare at her, and it made everything inside her light up.

"Boone, I want you."

He let out a low groan, then leaned forward. Then his warm mouth closed on one of her nipples, and he sucked.

Now, the room filled with Gemma's moans. Sensations poured through her. She undulated and slid her hands into his hair. She pulled him closer.

It felt *so* good.

"More," she panted.

He switched to the other breast, tugging her closer. She felt the hard bulge beneath her, and moved her hips, rubbing against him. It felt so good to think of nothing but pure desire. How much she wanted this good, protective man.

"Oh, my God." Her head fell back, her fingers tangling in the brown strands of his hair. She rubbed against that rock-hard cock beneath her, and wondered what it looked like. What it would feel like inside her.

"*Boone*," she moaned.

Suddenly, he moved. He stood and dumped her on her feet. She felt dizzy for a second and gripped the vanity to catch her balance. He stared at her for a beat, no emotion on his face.

"This is wrong."

She frowned. It wasn't wrong. Nothing had ever felt this right. "Boone—"

A muscle ticked in his jaw. "I won't take advantage of you."

She huffed out a breath. "You're *not*. My eyes are

wide open right now." More than they had been in a long time. "I know what I'm feeling."

He sucked in a breath. "I'm not the man for you. I'm not the man for anyone." He opened the door, stepped out, and closed it behind him.

Gemma crouched and snatched up her towel. Goosebumps washed over her as she wrapped it around herself.

The man had a hard shell around him that was inches thick. It was like he couldn't accept pleasure, or anything nice, or anyone caring.

Like he didn't think he deserved it.

She looked at her reflection in the mirror. Did she want to change that?

It was a hell of a time to find a guy who made her feel more than she'd felt in a really long time.

"One step at a time, Gemma."

But right then and there, she decided she wasn't giving up on Boone Hendrix.

GEMMA'S EYES SNAPPED OPEN, her heart racing. She sat up. The room was dark, and she was disoriented. Where was she?

Then she heard a low groan echo in the dark room.

"No. No. *Stop*."

Boone's voice. Her heart hit her ribs.

She heard a low whine and saw the shadow of Atlas pacing between the beds, agitated.

Boone thrashed on his bed.

She glanced at the glow of the alarm clock. They'd gone to sleep a few hours ago.

She bit her lip. "Boone? Boone?"

"Stop! Don't hurt him. Take me."

Raw pain tore through her. The agony in his voice was horrible. She hurt for him. For the memories that still haunted him.

She swung her legs over the side of the bed, but was careful not to get too close to him.

"Boone, you're having a nightmare." She reached out and touched his bare shoulder. "You're safe."

He went still.

"Are you awake?" she asked.

"Yes." His voice was hoarse. "I'm—"

"Don't you dare apologize."

She heard his harsh expulsion of breath.

"You need some water?"

"No."

She set her shoulders back. She wouldn't let him suffer alone because he was being stubborn. "Move over."

"What?"

She lifted the covers on his bed. "I'm coming in."

"Gemma." The word was a growl. "This is a bad idea."

She slid in. "No, it's not. Don't worry, I won't take advantage of you, Boone."

With both of them in it, the bed sagged a little, and she slid into the center, colliding with his hard body. He wasn't wearing a shirt, and all she felt was warm skin.

Oh. Her belly clenched. She hoped she wasn't lying when she said she wouldn't take advantage of him.

She settled her head on his arm. "Cuddling helps keep nightmares away."

His body was stiff. "You have nightmares?"

"I used to when I was younger." She paused. "My mom used to stay with me. I'd forgotten that."

He started to relax a little.

"I'm sorry your friends' deaths haunt you." Silence stretched and she stifled a sigh. "You must miss them."

"Yeah. Every day."

The darkness wrapped around them, and she surreptitiously rubbed her cheek against his arm.

"I watched them die."

Gemma sucked in a breath and held it. She stayed quiet and waited for him to go on. She couldn't see his face, but she felt the tension in him. She turned her face into him, pressing into him more firmly. She knew the darkness made it easier to talk.

His arm curled around her, holding her tight.

"I'm here, Boone. I'm listening."

She wanted to know what haunted him, what hurt him. She wanted to hear it, so she could share it and help him let it go.

"Our team had split up. I was with my friends Julio, Miles, and Charlie." His next breath was ragged. "We were ambushed. A fierce group of Taliban fighters took us hostage, put us in a cell."

His heart was racing. She smoothed a hand over his bare chest. His breathing sped up.

She wanted to comfort him, tell him it was okay. But she knew that wasn't what he needed right now.

"They wanted intel." Another fast breath. "They

took Miles first." He shook his head. "They strung him up and tortured him. I still hear his screams."

She squeezed her eyes closed. "I'm sorry."

"They beheaded him in front of us." His tone was wooden. "They took Charlie next."

Gemma bit back a sob. She had to be strong enough for him, to help him. She held him tighter.

"I begged them to take me. Miles was engaged. Charlie had a pretty wife. Julio had kids. I had no one, and I wanted them to take me."

Her hero. Ready to sacrifice himself.

"One of them held a gun to Julio's head, yelling in Arabic. Taunting me because there wasn't a damn thing I could do." He dragged in a harsh breath. "After they killed Julio, they were getting ready to torture me. That's when Vander and the rest of our team arrived." His hand moved into her hair. "Mostly, I don't understand why I made it back and they didn't."

She rubbed her cheek against his warm skin. "That's a decision above all our pay grades. Life is life, Boone. Good things happen, bad things happen. We like to think we have control over it, but we don't."

"They had wives, kids. Kids who don't have a father now."

"If you hadn't made it back, you wouldn't have been able to rescue me. I'm grateful for that."

She felt him stroke her hair.

"I'm glad, too."

Suddenly, the bed dipped under another weight as Atlas jumped on.

"*Atlas*," Boone growled.

"He was worried about you."

The dog licked Boone's face, fur tickling her face. She felt a smile curl her lips. Then Atlas dropped down and settled in beside her.

Gemma was now pinned in by the Hendrix males.

She liked it.

"Sleep now," she said, softly.

He buried his face in her hair, and she closed her eyes and held on tight.

CHAPTER NINE

"Pick something."

Gemma whirled. "Boone, this isn't something that can be rushed."

He'd woken early, with Gemma wrapped around him and his cock so hard it had been agony.

Eventually, he'd slid out of the bed and left her snuggled up with Atlas. He'd taken a quick shower, and jerked off, remembering the sounds she'd made when he tasted her sweet nipples.

But Gemma Newhouse didn't just make him hard. She made him...feel. She'd listened as he'd poured out the festering pain inside him. She'd held him tight, helped ease that constant churn he felt inside.

This morning, she hadn't looked at him any differently. She'd smiled at him as she'd dressed and given him a quick kiss before they'd set off.

Boone still felt a little raw. Kept expecting her to look at him like...

Shit. He didn't know. He ran a hand through his hair.

The truth was, she was exactly the same as she'd been yesterday. Sweet, smiling Gemma.

They'd driven for a few hours and had just stopped at a bakery to grab some breakfast. Except apparently Gemma needed to examine *every* baked good numerous times, before she'd make her decision.

"The muffins look good." She tapped a finger against her lips. "But I bet the cinnamon rolls are delicious."

"So get both."

"Both will go to my already ample hips."

His gaze dropped. "I don't see that as a problem."

She smiled at him and turned back to the glass case. "Ooh, there are scones, too."

Boone stepped up behind her. "We'll have one of everything she just said, and a doughnut. And one black coffee, and a cappuccino. All to go."

The woman behind the counter smiled. "A man who knows how to keep his woman happy."

Gemma slid her arm through his. "Oh, he does." She lowered her voice. "If he'd listen to the woman, and give her *everything* she wanted." There was heat in her gaze.

"Behave."

"Maybe I'm tired of behaving. That hasn't exactly worked out for me in the past. The best thing I did was go on *Cake and Bake*, and that wasn't behaving. Or at least, according to my parents."

He gave her ass a light swat. "Misbehaving gets you in trouble."

She arched a brow. "Trouble sounds good to me."

He wanted to kiss her. He let his gaze run over her

pretty face and those freckles. It wasn't just the face that tempted him, or the sweet body.

Gemma cared. She felt deeply. She'd comforted him after his nightmare and his confession. And she didn't look at him like he was weird, or broken, or weak.

"Here you go." The woman held out a white paper bag. "Enjoy."

Gemma took it. "Oh, we will."

Atlas was waiting in the truck. Boone had already fed him, but the dog sniffed the bag, nuzzling the paper.

"These aren't for you, handsome," Gemma said. "As soon as I can, I'll bake some more dog treats for you."

Boone's dog gave Gemma an adoring look. He was pretty sure Atlas was half in love with her.

Soon they were back on the road. If they had a good run, they should make Denver by the afternoon.

Gemma handed him a donut, and he ate it while Gemma ate her muffin. She sang along to some sickly-sweet pop song that came on the radio.

Boone smiled. She didn't have a bad voice, but she wasn't exactly in tune. She made up for it with her enthusiasm.

The highway stretched ahead. It had been a while since he'd driven such a long distance. He glanced at Gemma, who was serenading Atlas. It was nice to take a trip with company. A woman filled with light and life. She was fighting off the weight of expectations to follow her passion, and she was being hunted by dangerous people, but she was still smiling.

He glanced in the rearview mirror.

Then he stiffened.

Two black SUVs were bearing down on them. Fast.

His instincts started screaming.

"Gemma, you strapped in?"

Her singing cut off. "Of course. Who doesn't wear a seatbelt in this day and age?" Then she frowned, picking up on his tension. "What's wrong?"

"We have company."

She gasped and looked back. "How? How did they find us?"

A good fucking question.

"Stay down." He stomped on the accelerator.

As he picked up speed, so did the SUVs.

One roared up beside them. The windows were tinted, and he couldn't see inside. Then suddenly, the SUV careened into them. Metal crunched. Gemma screamed.

Boone held tight, fighting to keep them on the road. Then he jerked the wheel, ramming his truck into the SUV.

"God, we're going to die," she cried.

"Not today." Jaw tight, he rammed the SUV again. It lost control and careened off the road.

In the rearview mirror, he saw it flip.

"Oh, shit," Gemma panted.

"Stay down."

Bullets peppered the back of his truck. Boone ducked, and Gemma screamed again. Atlas stayed low, and didn't make a sound or move. Boone leaned over him, opened the glove box, and pulled out a handgun.

There was more gunfire, and suddenly the truck shuddered. Dammit, they'd hit a tire. He set the gun on the seat beside him, and gripped the wheel to stay in control.

Suddenly, Gemma opened her window.

"Gemma, what are you doing? I said stay down."

"No." She grabbed the handgun. "I'm going to help."

"*Gemma*," he growled.

He couldn't stop her and keep control of the truck at the same time.

She leaned out the window, aiming back at the SUV. She fired.

And kept firing. It was clear she'd used a gun before.

Suddenly, the SUV behind them swerved and came to a stop. She'd hit something, or someone.

Boone didn't slow down. He grabbed her and pulled her back inside.

She dropped back into the seat and closed the window. "Holy cow."

She was shaking.

He gripped her arm. "Next time, you listen to me."

"I'm fine, Boone."

He gritted his teeth. The idea of her hurt and bleeding...

She reached over Atlas and touched his stubbled cheek. "I'm okay. Now, let's get far away from here."

SHE COULDN'T STOP SHAKING.

Boone had pulled off the highway and ended up down a side road. They pulled into some trees and stopped.

"You need to change the tire, right?" Gemma asked.

"Right." He got out.

She opened her door, and Atlas jumped out. Gemma followed him, her legs feeling like jelly.

She took a step from the truck. *You're fine. You and Boone are safe. You weren't a victim. You fought back.*

Boone circled the truck, his face like thunder.

Uh-oh. She stilled.

"You should *never* have opened the window and put yourself in the line of fire."

She lifted her chin. "You're welcome. I got them off us."

"You put yourself in danger." He closed the gap between them and pinned her against the side of the truck.

Gemma found herself caught between cool metal and a hard, angry man. "It worked out, Boone. My father's security team taught me to shoot. It was the only way I could convince my father I didn't need a bodyguard once I finished college." She cupped his cheek. "We're both alive."

He made a growling sound and then his mouth crashed down on hers.

Her mouth opened instantly, and she let him in. Their tongues tangled. She pressed into him, desire white hot inside her. One of his hands clenched in her hair, tilting her mouth for his. The kiss was a savage assault, a battle, and she didn't know if she wanted to win or lose.

His name was like a chant inside her head, mixed up with the intense need. His hands were all over her, sliding under her sweater, and he pressed hard against her. She felt the rigid line of his cock against her.

Yes, God, yes. All the worry and fear changed into desire. She needed this. She needed him.

"Boone, please."

He tore her jeans open and one hand slid in. She bucked against him. His finger slid right under the elastic of her panties and touched her slick flesh. She was already soaking wet for him.

He growled. "Gemma, damn." He pulled his hand out, his eyes burning. He licked his finger. "God, you smell good." His hungry gaze met hers. "I have to taste you."

Her belly clenched. "Yes. *Yes.*"

He hoisted her up and set her on the hood of the truck. She sucked in some fast breaths, watching as he stripped her jeans and panties off with quick, jerky movements.

So sexy. She vaguely registered warm metal under her ass, but all she could see was the hungry man. She clenched her thighs together, but he pushed them apart.

"Got to get my mouth on your pretty pussy, Gemma."

The dirty talk made heat arrow through her. "*Yes.*"

But first, he peppered kisses along her thigh, paying special attention to any fading bruises and healing scratches he found. His lips moved across her belly, then found the still-angry scratch on her hip. He kissed it gently.

Gemma moaned.

Then he gripped her knees, hauling her closer, and pressed his face between her legs.

She cried out, body arching. He made a deep, masculine sound and proceeded to eat her. She moaned as he licked her, then he flicked his tongue over her clit.

Oh. God.

He kept her spread wide, his hands sliding under her ass, holding her to his mouth. His clever tongue and mouth, lapping, licking and sucking. She couldn't hold back her cries. The things he was doing to her...she'd never, ever had a man please her like this before. Like he was a little wild, a little desperate, like he couldn't get enough of her.

She moaned, one hand sliding into his hair. She pulled him closer. "Oh, crap, Boone..."

She felt her orgasm coiling up inside her, ready to burst. He growled against her sensitive flesh and sucked on her clit.

"Don't stop," she cried.

He sucked harder.

One second, there was frantic need, and the next, she was flying. She screamed, the pleasure hitting her hard. She'd never come like this before.

She collapsed back on the hood, her legs clenched on Boone. She looked down at his dark head and watched as he licked her inner thigh. She quivered. His golden gaze met hers.

"Better than your chocolate cake."

Gemma laughed. They were both panting, staring at each other.

He straightened and cupped her face in his big hands. "You won't put yourself in danger again."

"I will if it helps you. And if that earthshattering

orgasm was supposed to deter me, you've got things very, very wrong."

His lips twitched, his fingers sliding up into her hair. "You're too damn brave."

"I never have been before. But I won't let these people kill me or you. Or Atlas."

Responding to his name, the dog trotted over and nudged Boone's legs.

"Oh, God, don't let him see me," Gemma cried.

"He's a dog."

"I don't care!"

Shaking his head, Boone snatched up her jeans and panties off the ground, dusted them off, then handed them to her. "I'll change the tire."

"I'll help." She wiggled into her jeans, making sure Atlas wasn't getting an eyeful. Thankfully, the dog was off sniffing around.

As Boone got the spare tire out, Gemma grabbed the jack and got it ready. Boone loosened the lugs with a wrench and eyed her.

"You know how to change a tire?"

She rolled her eyes. "What, you think it's too much for a billionaire heiress?"

"I think you are nothing like I expected and full of surprises."

She felt a flush fill her cheeks. "Thank you. And it's another skill my dad's security team instilled in me." She got the jack in place.

That's when she noticed the bullet holes peppering the tailgate of his truck. Her throat tightened. The explosive orgasm and being with Boone had made her forget for a minute.

"Hey." He stroked a hand down her arm. "Those can be fixed."

She nodded, but she knew bullet holes in a person were a completely different thing. Boone was becoming important to her, and the idea of him getting shot protecting her was something her brain refused to contemplate.

She suspected he'd already been shot at enough in his life.

Soon Boone was maneuvering the spare tire into position. She had to admit that there was something sexy about watching a man change a tire.

After the tire was on, Boone dropped to the ground and slid under the truck.

"What are you doing?"

"Checking for any trackers."

She frowned at his jean-clad legs. "They can't have a tracker on this truck."

He grunted and slid out. He circled the truck, crouching down to check under the wheel well. "I'm worried about how the hell they tracked us so quickly."

"Maybe they got lucky? Got a hit on facial rec somewhere."

"Maybe."

Once he was satisfied there were no trackers, they got back on the road. Boone stuck to the smaller roads, avoiding the highway.

After an hour, they stopped at a small gas station. Gemma hung out with Atlas, while Boone spoke with

ANNA HACKETT

Vander on a pay phone. But she kept sneaking glances at him.

What he'd done to her on his truck...? She bit her bottom lip and pressed her thighs together. Even with all the danger around them, even with people hunting them, she wanted him to do it again.

She wanted Boone's hands on her. She wanted to explore that tough, hard body of his.

She watched him stride back to the truck and forced her little fantasies under control. His face was blank, his jaw tight.

"Any news?"

"Yes. Your father wants to talk with you."

Her pulse jumped, and she hurried over to the pay phone. She lifted the receiver. "Hello?"

"Gem? God, are you all right?"

Her father's worried voice made her chest tighten. "I'm okay, Dad."

"Your mother and I have been so worried."

Through the line, she heard her mother sob. "It's been pretty scary, but I'm alive. I'm not hurt. Are you two all right?"

"We're fine, honey. We're back in LA."

She lifted her gaze. "I got very lucky when Boone found me."

"Vander has sung the man's praises. We can't thank him enough. Look, I've sent a full security team and a jet. They'll be waiting for you when you reach Denver."

Gemma's hand tightened on the phone. "Oh?" In just a few hours, she'd be whisked away. Away from danger.

Away from Boone.

The emotions that hit her were stronger than she expected. She hadn't known Boone long.

This was safest for everyone. For her, and for Boone. There would be no one shooting at his truck or attacking him if she were back in California.

God, she hadn't expected this to hurt so much.

"Stick with Hendrix, Gemma. He'll get you to the jet. This will all be over soon."

"Okay, Dad." Her voice was thick.

"Gemma...I know I don't tell you enough, but I love you. You'll always be my baby girl."

Now her eyes filled with tears. "I love you too, Dad. And tell Mom as well."

"We'll see you soon."

She hung up the phone, then turned to face Boone. He had his hands in the pockets of his jeans.

"So, my father's sent a jet."

Boone gave a quick nod. "Vander briefed me. We need to get to Denver as fast as we can, but stay off any major highways."

He sounded like one of her father's security team. Cool, detached, professional.

Pain wound around her chest. "Okay."

"It'll take us a little longer, but it'll be safer. We'll be there this evening, and I'll take you straight to the airport."

His voice was devoid of any emotion. Did he care? Kisses and hot moments aside, maybe he was glad to get rid of her. "Right. Did Vander say anything else?"

"Just that he and his team are still tracking who hired the mercenaries. Nothing more, yet."

They headed back toward the truck.

"Gemma?"

She jerked her head up.

Something moved across his face, like he wanted to say something. Then he shook his head and opened the door for her.

Gemma tried to put on a brave face as Atlas jumped inside. "So, who's in charge of picking the tunes next?" She climbed in.

Boone slid behind the wheel. "Me." He reached over and changed it to a country station.

"Nooo." She slapped a hand to her forehead. "These songs are always about the heartbroken man and his truck."

He started the engine. "I know. Real music."

She smiled, even though she felt a strange emptiness growing inside her.

Soon, this would be over.

Atlas dropped his head in her lap, and she rubbed between his ears. Both the dog and the man were going to make it very hard to say goodbye.

CHAPTER TEN

Taking the back roads added time. Night had fallen by the time they neared Denver. The city glowed in the distance, dwarfed by the shadows of the mountains behind it.

Gemma saw the signs for Denver Airport and felt like there was a rock in her stomach. Growing heavier with every mile.

She cleared her throat. "I can't thank you enough for everything, Boone. Without you—" She shook her head. "I wouldn't have made it."

"You're stronger than you give yourself credit for."

His words filled her with warmth. But he wasn't looking at her. Instead he stared straight through the windshield, hands clamped on the steering wheel.

The air in the truck was thick and tense. She twisted her hands together. She had no right to feel this bereft about leaving him.

"I'm sure you'll be glad to be rid of me."

Suddenly, he wrenched the wheel and pulled off on the side of the road.

Gemma gasped, and Atlas raised his head.

Boone reached over and opened her door. "Atlas, explore."

The dog happily complied and jumped out. Boone stayed in her personal space, his chest rising and falling fast.

"There is *no* time or place where I'd be happy to be rid of you." His tone was low, lethal.

She sucked in a breath. She wasn't sure who moved first, him or her. It didn't matter. In the next second, Gemma was on his lap, straddling him.

They clutched at each other, mouths clashing. She slid her hands into his hair to drag his mouth closer, while his hands dug into her ass. Her heartbeat was thundering hard, and all she could do was lose herself in the raw sensation. There was only Boone, and there was nothing between them.

She didn't want the kiss to stop. Ever.

Then he bit down on her bottom lip, dragging a moan out of her. He broke the kiss, and she felt the harsh pants of his breath against her lips. He pressed his forehead against hers.

"I don't want to leave," she whispered.

"I don't want you to leave."

"But I know it's safer for you."

He made a sound. "It's not my safety I care about."

She met his gaze. "But I do. Boone, I do."

He cupped the side of her face. "Gemma, I've been broken for a long time."

She bit her lip. She knew he believed that. That he'd been shattered in that cell, watching his friends die. "Not broken, Boone. Bent, cracked, beaten, but not broken."

He stroked her cheekbone. "You actually make me believe that." He blew out a breath. "The safest thing is for you to get on that jet."

Sadness filled her. "I know."

"After all this is over, then...we'll see."

It wasn't a promise, but it was something. A part of her was deathly afraid that after she was gone, and once he was back in Vermont, he'd forget about her. Too many people in her life had always found her lacking.

He pressed a firm kiss to her lips. "Let's go, or we'll be late."

She settled back in her seat while Boone called for Atlas.

They were quiet as they passed through the security check at the gate, and drove into the quiet corner of the airport where the private jet hangers were located.

She recognized the Expanse jet out on the tarmac. There were several men in suits standing at the base of the stairs.

Boone drove in slowly and stopped.

"I guess this is it." She tried to sound cheery. "Bye, Atlas." As she gave the dog a vigorous final pat, Atlas whined softly.

Boone climbed out, circled the truck, and opened her door. She saw him eyeing her dad's men. She recognized a couple of them.

Gold-brown eyes met hers. "Stay safe."

"You too." Her throat was so tight it was hard to talk.

She'd just stepped out of the truck when she heard the crack of a gunshot.

Then another.

Gemma blinked and saw two of the security guards fall.

"Sniper!" Boone yelled.

The truck window on the passenger side shattered, showering them with glass. Boone dragged her down, covering her with his body.

There were more gunshots, and she heard the squeal of tires. She glanced up and saw a black SUV speeding toward them.

"*In.*" Boone shoved her into the truck. Atlas growled, staying low. "Stay down." Boone shoved past her, sliding across the seats, and got behind the wheel.

There was more gunfire. The back window of the truck shattered, and Boone cursed.

The engine started, and they sped forward. He yanked the wheel, the tires screeching as they turned.

Gemma stayed in a tight ball with her head down. She had no idea what was happening. The last thing she wanted to do was distract Boone. She gripped Atlas' fur and held on.

Boone kept driving. Eventually, there was no more gunfire.

"You can sit up."

Gingerly, she sat up and saw they were on the road heading away from the airport. She felt shaky and pressed a hand to her chest. "Are they following us?"

"I lost them. Open the glove box for me. There's a clean burner phone in there. Hand it to me."

His voice was clipped, and she knew he was in fight mode. She pulled out the cellphone and handed it to him.

He held it to his ear. "Vander, we were ambushed at the airport. Some of Newhouse's security team were killed. Yeah, she's okay." There was a pause. "Okay." Another pause. "Roger that. I will." He ended the call and glanced her way. "Vander has a contact in Denver who can help us. They'll give us a clean vehicle and supplies."

Gemma was pretty sure Boone's idea of supplies meant weapons.

His gaze locked on hers. "You're staying with me."

BOONE HAD BEEN to Denver a few times and knew the roads pretty well. As he drove into the city center, he kept checking the mirrors for a tail.

Beside him, Gemma seemed all right. Although, he noted, she kept a hand clenched on Atlas. Her courage amazed him. He knew most people would have crumpled under the stress of her situation by now.

"Who's this friend of Vander's that we're meeting?" Gemma asked.

"A security firm. They usually provide security for archeological digs and expeditions. They're called Treasure Hunter Security."

"I wanted to be an archeologist when I was young. Finding lost temples and fabulous treasures."

Boone snorted. "I think that usually only happens in the movies."

"Well, Dad steered me away from studying history."

Boone frowned. He was starting to think he didn't like Paul Newhouse very much.

Finally, he neared the address Vander had given him in the lower downtown area of Denver. LoDo had a lot of renovated historic warehouses and was home to Union Station and the baseball stadium.

He turned into a narrow alley and then stopped. He cut the lights. "This is the place."

"Now what?" she asked.

"Someone's going to meet us." As he got out, he glanced around and didn't see any CCTV cameras. He helped Gemma out of the truck.

A man emerged from the shadows. He was tall and fit, wearing tan cargo pants and a black Henley.

Boone tensed, ready to go for his Glock.

"Hendrix?"

Boone nodded. "Call me Boone. You're Declan Ward?"

"Yeah." The man walked closer and held out a hand. They shook.

Boone could have picked the guy as a former Navy SEAL in a heartbeat, even if Vander hadn't already told him. "This is Gemma."

Declan nodded. "Heard you've had a rough few days."

Gemma pulled a face. "That's the understatement of the year."

Declan's lips twitched. "I've had a few days like that myself. Come on." He paused as Atlas leaped out of the truck. "Who is this?"

"My dog, Atlas."

"He's a good-looking dog." Declan met Boone's gaze. "And looks well-trained."

"He is, but he's retired, so he isn't above begging for food or back scratches."

Declan chuckled. "Grab anything you need. I'll have one of my team take care of your truck."

"The people after Gemma will be looking for us, and they've proved to be damn good at tracking us down. They clearly have resources."

The other man nodded. "Don't worry. We'll take care of it, and my tech whiz has been scrubbing security feed of you driving into LoDo. These guys won't be able to find you."

"Thank you," Gemma said quietly.

They followed Declan onto the street and walked one block over. Boone noted the path the man took avoided any cameras. He led them to a building that looked like it had once been an old factory, but now had lots of big windows that no doubt gave a good view of the city and mountains in the daytime.

Declan held the door open for them. Inside, Atlas' claws clicked on the concrete floor. They passed an empty reception desk and stepped into a cavernous space. There was a conference table closest to them, some couches grouped around a large coffee table. By the bank of large windows sat a pool table and an air hockey table. Flat screens covered the far brick wall—most were dark at the moment, but a few were still filled with information. Desks sat in front of the screens, all covered in high-end computers.

A man who looked similar in build and looks to Declan leaned against one desk, a little girl with pigtails in his arms. There were two women with him. A tall woman with dark, curly hair stood close to his side, tickling the little girl. The other woman sat in a chair at a computer, her dark hair in a sleek cut that brushed her jaw line. She was busy tapping on the keyboard.

The man looked up as they approached.

"Guys," Declan said. "This is Boone and Gemma. Oh, and this is Atlas." He waved at the dog.

The man did a chin lift. "I'm Cal Ward."

Brothers. Boone knew that both men were former Navy SEALs, and from what Vander had shared, badasses.

The tall woman smiled. "I'm Dani Navarro-Ward, Cal's wife."

"Dani Navarro? The photographer?" Gemma clapped her hands together. "I have a framed picture of Angkor Wat you took at sunrise, hanging in my apartment. I love it."

The woman shared a brief smile with her husband. "I'm glad you like it. And you're Gemma Newhouse. I watched *Cake and Bake*. That red velvet cake you made in the finale was sensational."

Gemma smiled. "I can't take a decent picture to save my life, but I can bake a mean red velvet cake."

The woman in the chair swiveled. Her blue gaze was sharp and direct. "And I'm Darcy Burke. I used to be a Ward. Gemma, Vander's team brought us up to speed on everything you've been through. How are you holding up?"

"I'm feeling pretty lucky that I fell in Boone's river. Without him, I wouldn't have made it."

"I just finished removing any trace that your truck drove into LoDo. Should throw the mercenaries off your trail."

"Thank you," Gemma said.

The little girl in Cal's arms wriggled, her gaze on Atlas. "Doggie."

"And who are you, sweetie?" Gemma asked.

"I'm Emmy." She gave Gemma a shy smile.

Boone didn't have much experience with kids, so the best he could tell, Emmy was a few years old.

The girl held her hands out to Declan.

"Someone wants her daddy." Darcy smiled. "Her mom's away, so she gets clingy."

"My wife, Layne, is an archeologist," Declan said. "She's away on a dig for a week."

"Mama?" the little girl asked hopefully.

"She'll be home soon, sweetness." Declan kissed the top of her head. "Is it okay if she pats Atlas?"

"Sure," Boone said. "He'll love it."

Declan held the little girl while she patted the dog and beamed.

"She should be in bed," Dani added. "But she refused until Declan could do the honors."

"Which will be very soon." Declan expertly set the little girl on his hip, and she snuggled against his shoulder. "Boone, we have a couple of clean cellphones for you and Gemma, as well as a secure laptop. And some weapons and gear."

"Thank you," Boone said.

ANNA HACKETT

"And I have this for you." Darcy held up a small device. "It'll create a secure hotspot for you that can't be traced."

"I can offer you the apartment upstairs, if you need a place to stay," Declan added.

Boone shook his head. "I've got a friend in the mountains. We're going up there."

Declan nodded. "Remote, and out of sight. Good choice. There are too many cameras in the city."

"And these guys have already tracked us twice since we've been on the road. Not giving them another chance."

A computer pinged and Darcy whirled, then tapped on the keyboard. "Guys, Vander just sent some intel." She looked up, her blue gaze sharp. "He's identified who hired the mercenaries who are after Gemma."

Boone stiffened.

Gemma gasped. "Who?"

"A multimillionaire English businessman by the name of William Barron Carruthers."

Declan and Cal both cursed.

"You know him?" Boone asked.

"Yeah," Declan said. "Carruthers runs some legitimate businesses, but he's well known in the right circles for selling arms."

"An arms dealer?" Gemma sounded horrified.

"Carruthers is high-end," Cal added. "He doesn't pedal guns and grenades. He only does big stuff. Drones, missiles, high-tech systems."

"Carruthers owns a vast estate in Vermont," Darcy

112

added. "I suspect that's where your abductors were taking you when you escaped.

"What could he want with me?" Gemma said. "I can assure you that my father's company does not have anything to do with weaponry. Expanse specializes in online retail and cloud storage."

"We'll work it out," Boone said. "And then we'll expose the asshole."

"Vander said to remind you that your mission priority is keeping her safe," Declan said.

Boone nodded and took Gemma's hand. "I haven't forgotten."

CHAPTER ELEVEN

"Y ou like Mexican food?"

Gemma glanced at Boone as he drove them through Denver. Her mind was still spinning after the attack at the airport and learning that an international arms dealer was after her.

"Who the hell is this Carruthers, Boone? I can't wrap my head around this. Nothing Expanse does should interest him."

He reached over and gripped her knee. "It's going to be okay. Once we get to the mountains, we have the laptop from Declan. We can do a little digging of our own on Carruthers."

Okay, that would help. Doing anything was better than just feeling like a sitting duck with a target painted on her back.

"So, Mexican food?" Boone asked again.

She drew in a deep breath and tried to relax. They were in a new vehicle the THS team had given them. The Jeep Cherokee was dark green, a few years old, and best of all, the mercenaries had no idea they were driving it. "Sure, I like Mexican food. One word. Cheese. After sugar, it's a favorite thing of mine."

"We'll grab some Mexican takeout for dinner."

She cleared her throat. "Actually, there's a bakery I'd love to visit. After the last few days, I need to stock up on comfort food. There's one in LA but I don't get to it often enough."

Boone smiled and shook his head. "Is it open this late?"

"It just so happens that it is. They make these *incredible* doughnuts." She tapped on her new cellphone. "Looks like there's a decent Mexican restaurant nearby, as well. Lots of good reviews."

"Burritos and doughnuts it is. Give me the address."

She beamed at him. "Thanks, Boone."

They had a plan. The Treasure Hunter Security gang had given them a Jeep and supplies. They'd grab their food and then disappear into the mountains.

"Does your friend know we're coming?"

"Yeah. I gave him a call. I almost didn't. Sometimes it's best just to surprise Shep. He's not the most social guy."

"Another loner."

"Yeah, but he makes me look extroverted. Anti-social tendencies aside, Shep's a damn good man. I've seen him risk his life, again and again, to do what's right. To save his fellow soldiers, or rescue women and children. He doesn't mind disobeying an order if he has to. Used to drive Vander crazy."

"I can't imagine Vander losing his cool."

"No. He hides it pretty well. We'd only know when he'd chew Shep out after a mission was done." Boone found a parking spot near the bakery. "But Vander always protected him from the brass."

All these heroes. Willing to put themselves on the line for others.

Gemma looked out the window, then saw the Voodoo Doughnut sign, and grinned. The store was painted signature hot pink and well-lit. Beside her, Atlas stirred.

"This place started in Oregon, and they have a bunch of stores across the country. They make artisan doughnuts, like the Vicious Hibiscus, Mango Tango, and the Bacon Maple Bar, to name a few."

"I'm starting to feel nervous."

She laughed, and felt some of the tension in her shoulders ease. "I'll get a mixed dozen and we can try a bunch of flavors."

Boone parked and gave Atlas a brisk rub. "You stay here." He opened the window for the dog. "We'll be back soon."

She looked up and down the street, anxiety tickling her chest. She couldn't easily shake the knowledge she was being hunted.

Boone took her hand and squeezed it. She felt some of that tension melt away.

Despite the late hour, Voodoo Doughnut had a decent crowd. Gemma smiled, taking in the pink walls and the display cases filled with brightly decorated doughnuts.

"I'll get the takeout and come back to you," Boone said. "Do not leave the store."

She saluted.

He shook his head. "That's a terrible salute. I'll have to show you how to do it properly."

She watched him leave. The man sure was built and knew how to make a pair of jeans look amazing. She saw a few other women in the bakery watching him, too.

She nibbled her lip. There was something she was starting to like almost as much as she liked sugar—Boone Hendrix.

After all this was over, maybe she could convince him to spend some time together.

Without the bad guys hunting them.

Gemma ordered her doughnuts. There were so many fun combinations. She vowed to try making a few unexpected things of her own when she got back to her baking. Mix things up a bit.

And she was going to open her own bakery. A jittery shiver ran through her and she grinned. She'd survived an abduction and several gun fights. Starting a bakery should be a breeze. She was also going to ask her dad to help with her business plan.

Like Boone had said, life was far too short to keep putting things off.

"Here you go." The man behind the counter handed her a pink box of doughnuts with a wide smile.

"Thanks."

"Enjoy the sugar overload."

"Oh, I plan to."

She stood by the door, and through the glass window, she saw Boone coming back toward her, a takeout bag in one hand. He was scanning the street and looked tense and alert.

She met him at the door. "Everything okay?"

"I thought I spotted someone watching us."

Gemma stiffened and glanced down the sidewalk.

"The guy moved on," Boone said. "Maybe it was nothing."

But clearly this guy had set off Boone's radar. Her chest tightened.

"Let's go." He pressed a hand to her lower back, and they headed toward the truck.

Gemma moved quickly. The sooner they were in the mountains, the better. She felt so exposed right now.

She was so glad she had Boone with her.

They passed the mouth of an alley, and the rotting scent from a dumpster made her wrinkle her nose.

Suddenly, a shadow detached from the wall and charged at Boone.

She cried out. Boone shoved her out of the way, and she dropped the box of doughnuts. It hit the pavement with a slap. The takeout bag hit the ground as well.

She swiveled and watched a tall man take a swing at Boone.

Oh, God.

Boone blocked the man's hit, then rammed his fist into the man's midsection. Next, his elbow snapped up and connected with the man's jaw.

The attacker staggered. Boone didn't stop. He moved so fast she could barely make out all the blows.

Punch. Hit. Elbow.

With a groan, the man collapsed on the dirty

concrete. Boone stood over him, hands clenched into tight fists.

Boone had done it so easily. He'd taken the man down without even breaking a sweat.

"Come on." He swiveled and gripped her upper arm.

"My doughnuts—"

"Leave them." Then he stiffened.

Gemma turned her head. Two men were striding toward them. She looked in the other direction. Another man, with a hard, blank face, was closing in.

How had these assholes found them? Fear coalesced into a hard ball in her stomach.

Boone pulled her back a step. "Gemma, run."

"What?"

"Run. Down the alley. Find a way out, then contact Declan at Treasure Hunter Security."

Leave him behind? Outnumbered with dangerous men? "Boone—"

He shoved her. "Go! Or we'll both be in danger."

Spinning, Gemma sprinted into the dark alley. Behind her, she heard a sharp whistle, then the sound of fighting.

Choking back a sob, she kept running.

THEY CAME AT HIM FAST.

Boone punched the first attacker, gripped the man's shirt, then spun. He slammed the man headfirst into the brick wall of the nearby building.

He sensed a second attacker launching at him, and

Boone swiveled and dodged. He narrowly avoided a slashing knife.

Boone's focus narrowed. He'd always enjoyed hand-to-hand combat. Looking his opponent in the eye.

He met the gaze of his attacker and bared his teeth. *Bring it, asshole.*

Boone pushed his worry for Gemma aside. Protecting her. That was all that mattered.

The next man rushed him. Boone threw his arm up and blocked the man's hit. He followed through with a palm to the face. The guy let out a choked sound and Boone hit him again. Then he rammed a kick into the man's gut.

The guy dropped to his knees. Boone lifted his boot and kicked the man over.

Heaving in air, he heard the scrape of a boot on concrete.

He was already whirling and caught a glimpse of another guy swinging a baton at him.

Without a sound, Atlas sailed through the air and leaped on the man. He'd heard Boone's whistle and gotten out of the truck.

"Fuck!" The guy dropped the baton, throwing his arms to protect himself from the snap of Atlas' jaws.

With a growl, the dog clamped onto the man's leg.

Boone punched him—once, twice. The man fell backward and hit the concrete.

They were all down.

"Atlas, release."

Then he heard Gemma's scream echo from deeper in the alley.

Adrenaline punched through him. *No.*

He took off at a sprint. He passed a reeking dumpster, then ahead, saw two shadowed silhouettes grappling in the dim light.

He whipped up his Glock.

There was enough light for him to see a tall man with a beard holding Gemma. He had a knife pressed against her throat.

The man saw Boone. "Stop there, or she's dead." He had a thick Romanian accent.

"We both know you need her alive, Radu."

"Drop your weapon." The man's tone was like ice. He pressed his knife to her cheek. "I may not kill her, but I can hurt her, leave her far less pretty."

Beside Boone, Atlas stood, alert and focused on Gemma's attacker.

The fear on her face was stark, and it cut at Boone. He was *not* letting her get hurt. He'd failed a lot of people in his life.

Not Gemma. Not today.

She met his gaze, and he barely controlled his jolt. She was scared, but she looked at him with pure trust in her eyes.

Suddenly, she stomped her foot down on the man's boot.

He growled, but loosened his hold enough that she half turned. And rammed her knee between the guy's legs. The man uttered a vicious curse.

"Gemma, down," Boone roared.

She didn't hesitate. She dropped instantly.

Boone fired.

The man's body jerked, and his knife fell from nerve-less fingers. He clutched his bleeding shoulder and hit the concrete on his ass.

"Gemma—"

Boone didn't need to say any more. She ran at him, and he caught her. But he didn't take his gaze off the man moaning on the ground.

"Are you hurt?" Boone asked her.

"No, I'm fine."

He tightened his grip on her. "We need to get—"

"You aren't going anywhere."

The deep voice behind them made Boone's jaw clench. They turned slowly, and he saw two more merce-naries. One was tall and lean, while the other one was shorter with a muscular build.

They were both armed with rifles.

Both aiming at Boone.

Gemma gasped, her hands digging into his arm.

"We're taking the girl," the tall man said.

This one had an American accent. He'd probably been military and now sold his services to the highest bidder. Boone couldn't stand the sight of him.

Atlas growled.

The other merc shifted his gun to aim at the dog.

"No!" Gemma stepped in front of Atlas.

Fuck. Boone didn't have a good play here. Not one that didn't put Gemma at risk.

"Come here." The tall guy gestured at Gemma.

She lifted her chin. "No. Tell Carruthers to get fucked."

The men traded a glance, then the tall one gave a

slow nod. "Then we'll have to put a bullet in your hero's head and drag you out of here."

She bit her lip.

All of a sudden, a shadow moved behind the men. Boone couldn't make out what it was, but he kept his face blank.

"I'll say it again," the merc repeated. "Come here."

The shadow moved closer, then attacked.

A blow to the back of the head sent the talking man toppling face-first to the dirty ground. He didn't move.

The second merc was turning, but didn't get a chance to defend himself. The newcomer slammed several heavy blows into the man.

The second mercenary went down hard.

Boone pulled Gemma toward him. Their rescuer took a step forward, and Boone noted the guy was big and broad. Then he stepped into a dim light and Boone saw a familiar dark beard covering a square jaw, and shaggy, black hair.

The man scowled at them. "This alley stinks."

"Shep," Boone said.

His friend grunted. "I've lost track of how many times I've saved your ass, Hendrix."

Atlas bounded over and licked the former Ghost Ops soldier's hand.

GEMMA'S PULSE was still racing, her heart hammering. She clutched Boone's arm like a lifeline.

He'd stormed in like some warrior—strong and

composed. Then she'd been terrified those men were going to shoot him and Atlas.

Now Boone's friend—who looked big, a little scary, and a lot grumpy—stood there pulling zip-ties from the pocket of his brown leather jacket.

"You have freakishly good timing," Boone said. "As always."

Shep grunted, then closed the distance between them. The men hugged, slapping each other's backs.

"Good to see you, Boone. Even if I did have to haul my ass into the city to find you. I hate the city."

"Shep, this is Gemma. Gemma, Shepherd Barlow."

"Hi." She held out a hand.

Shep took hers. He had a scarred, callused hand that was twice the size of hers. She felt his assessing gaze on her. "Glad you're okay."

Atlas leaned into her, and she ran a hand down the dog's back.

Shep's lips twitched. "I see Atlas has good taste."

Boone snorted. "That dog is a born flirt."

"Come on. I suggest we get back to my place as quickly as we can." He finished tying up the mercs. "I'll call a buddy at Denver PD to come and get these clowns."

The three of them made it back to the THS Jeep.

"I suggest we take mine," Shep said. "They could have a tracker on yours."

"They sure as hell seem to find us easily enough," Boone muttered. "We need to stay off any cameras as well."

"Come on." Shep whistled for Atlas.

They transferred their gear to Shep's big black Dodge Ram. Gemma sat in the backseat with Atlas, while the men talked in the front.

The pair had an easy camaraderie, and it made her smile. She was happy to see Boone had friends. As they drove toward the mountains, Shep placed a call to his cop friend.

Soon, they left the city behind them. The mountains were dark, and she wished she could see the view. The city lights of Denver behind them were pretty spectacular, though.

As they drove on, she found herself dozing. They left the highway, following the twists and turns of a road into the mountains. Shep followed a river for a bit before the road turned into dense trees. Finally, they turned and drove through a plain wooden gate.

The gravel road twisted higher up a hill. Then she saw a cabin with lights on up ahead, but she could see the shadows of several other buildings dotted around.

She leaned forward between the seats. "This is your place?"

"Yeah." Shep pulled to a stop and shut off the engine. "There's an old mine, as well. You'll see the old structure on the hill in the daytime. It was a silver mine during the boom in the late 1800s. It shut down decades ago. Then some rich guy bought the land to build these cabins. It was a fancy mountain getaway, and he rented the cabins out, but then he went bust. I bought it for a song while I was still in the military. I like the solitude and privacy."

Boone turned in his seat. "What he actually means is that Shep has a strong aversion to dealing with people."

The man grunted. "Only stupid people. Unfortunately, I find most people pretty stupid." He opened his door.

Once they were out, Atlas ran around, keen to explore. She smiled. This was the Colorado version of Boone's place, so the dog looked happy.

"I tidied up that cabin for you two." Shep pointed to the cabin closest to his. "I keep it maintained for guests."

"What guests?" Boone asked with a quirk of an eyebrow.

Shep shrugged. "Madden stayed here for a bit when he got out."

Boone nodded, and Gemma guessed they were talking about another Ghost Ops buddy.

"The fire's already going. And that's my place." He nodded his head at the well-lit cabin. "I figured after the last two days you guys have had, you have some sleep to catch up on."

"Yeah," Boone said. "Thanks, Shep."

"Oh, and the fridge is stocked as well."

"That's lucky, because we lost our takeout and our doughnuts." Gemma fought back a pout. She'd really wanted those doughnuts.

Shep flicked a glance at Gemma. "Food's not fancy."

She'd seen the look before and arched a brow. "And here I was expecting Beluga caviar and white truffles."

Her sarcasm had the corner of Shep's lips twitching. "I like her. I have a good security system, so you don't need to worry about anyone sneaking up on you."

Boone snorted. "Knowing you, the system's probably good enough to defend Fort Knox."

Boone's friend just inclined his head. "Not worth putting a crappy system in. I'll see you two in the morning."

"Thanks again, Shep." Boone lifted their bags and opened the cabin door.

Oh. Gemma took it all in. It was charming. There was lots of wood, a high ceiling, and a fire crackling happily in the stone fireplace. A comfy looking couch sat in front of the fire, and on the other side of the room were three doors that were all ajar. She moved closer to take a look. Two were bedrooms, both with big, wood-hewn beds. The final door led to a small bathroom. It looked a little dated, but there was a shower and a large tub, and it was clean.

It didn't have the cozy charm of Boone's Vermont cabin, but it was very comfortable.

"Hungry?" Boone opened the fridge.

"You know, I am now."

She watched him feed Atlas and pat his dog. She smiled. They were such a unit.

"How about sandwiches?" He held up a loaf of bread. "There's fresh bread, ham, and cheese."

"Sounds like heaven." She sank onto the couch.

Safe. They were safe. Finally, it was sinking in.

"People assume you have fancy taste." He set two plates with thick sandwiches on the coffee table, then sat beside her.

"I'm the daughter of a billionaire. It comes with the territory." She bit into her sandwich and moaned. When she looked up, Boone looked frozen, staring at her. "My life was pretty normal when I was young, while Dad was still building the business. Then I got to travel a lot. I like nice things. I've eaten at some of the world's best restaurants. Doesn't mean I don't know how to appreciate a good sandwich."

He nodded.

"Boone, thanks for saving me again. If you hadn't been there today..."

"You don't need to thank me."

"I know, but I am."

He lifted his sandwich. "Just eat."

CHAPTER TWELVE

B oone turned over in the bed. It was comfortable, and he should be asleep. He sighed. His door was ajar, and he could hear the crackle of the fire in the living room.

He was excruciatingly aware that Gemma was in the next room, wearing nothing but one of his T-shirts. He'd bought her some pajamas to wear, but for some reason, she'd still insisted on sleeping in his shirt.

Which he liked. Too damn much.

She'd practically fallen asleep halfway through her sandwich. The exhaustion and adrenaline crash had caught up with her.

Atlas made a soft noise. The dog was asleep on a rug on the floor.

With a huff, Boone turned over and punched his pillow. He should be tired after a long drive, and fighting off the mercenaries.

They were safe. Gemma was safe. And there was no way the assholes after her could find them here.

Instead of sleeping, there was only one thing—one woman—on his mind.

Earlier, he watched her smile as they'd eaten their simple dinner. The glow from the fire had danced over her skin. He'd wanted to count her freckles. See where else she had them on that curvy body of hers. He'd felt... content. The dark whispers in his head had gone silent.

What the hell was he doing? He had nothing to offer a woman like Gemma. A woman who was so bright, friendly, and clever.

He was broken, jaded. Hell, he lived alone in Vermont with his dog.

She deserved so much more.

And yet, the memories of the hungry way she'd kissed him were burned into his brain. As was the sweet taste of her pussy. Making her come, seeing her body shaking from the pleasure he'd given her, was something he'd never forget.

He groaned. His cock was as hard as a rock. He imagined her pressed against him, her hands moving over his gut, heading lower.

With a mental curse, he shoved his boxer shorts down. His hand circled his cock, and he gave it one rough pump.

Oh, fuck. He imagined Gemma touching him. Stroking him.

"Boone."

It took him a second to realize that Gemma's voice wasn't in his head. He quickly readjusted his boxer shorts and sat up.

He saw her silhouette in the bedroom doorway. She

was wearing a white T-shirt, her legs bare, her long, brown hair loose.

"You okay?"

"I can't sleep. I know I should be exhausted." Her hands fluttered.

"Go and sit by the fire. I'll make you some hot chocolate."

She nodded.

Clearly Atlas was tired. The dog raised his head for a millisecond, then went back to sleep.

Boone willed his cock to go down. The last thing he needed was Gemma seeing his boner. It took a minute, but he finally headed out. Gemma was pacing by the fire.

Damn, she was so beautiful.

She turned, and her gaze locked on his bare chest. She went still. "Oh. Um."

He arched a brow.

"You have so many muscles." She waved a hand.

"I'm sure you've seen muscles in LA."

"Yes, but not real ones. All those men are like glossy Ken dolls."

The way she was looking at him wasn't helping his cock behave.

She circled the couch and headed his way. "What's this?" She touched a circular scar on his chest.

Boone swallowed. "Old wound."

Her gaze met his. "A bullet wound?"

He nodded.

Her gaze moved over him, and he knew she was taking in all his old scars. He had an ugly knife wound on his side that had healed badly after it had gotten infected.

"I'll get started making the hot chocolate," he said.

"I don't want hot chocolate."

He stilled. "What do you want?"

"I want the bad guys to stop. I want to not be in danger."

He nodded. "I know, and—"

"And I want you."

Shit. "Gemma..."

"Don't give me the 'you're vulnerable' speech, Boone. You weren't worried about that when your mouth was..."

"Between your legs," he growled.

"Yes." She lifted her chin. "We're safe now. I know what I want." She pressed her hands to his chest.

He sucked in a sharp breath. Her hands were warm, and his body reacted. He could smell her fresh soap scent.

"And what exactly do you want?" His voice was low, husky.

"*You.* I want you to touch me. I want to touch you. I don't want to think about all the crap swirling around me. I want to feel something other than fear. I want you to make this ache go away."

Need vibrated through his body. He wasn't strong enough to resist her. It had been so long since he'd wanted anyone. And he'd never wanted a woman the way he wanted Gemma. "Gemma, you need to be sure."

"I'm sure."

With a low growl, he lifted her off her feet. He heard her gasp as he strode across the room and pinned her against the wall.

She gripped his shoulders, and eagerly wrapped her

legs around his hips. He felt the soft juncture of her thighs rub against his thickening cock.

He groaned.

"I want you, Boone," she murmured.

He fastened his mouth to hers. As soon as their lips met, he forgot all the reasons why he wasn't right for her.

Her tongue stroked his, her hands speared into his hair. She tugged hard.

He ground against her body, needing to get closer. He moved his mouth over hers, dragging in the taste of her.

She bit his lip. "Don't hold back."

He raked his teeth down the side of her neck and loved the breathy sound of her voice. But he also heard the solid certainty in her words.

"Tell me exactly what you want, Gemma? Spell it out for me."

Pretty hazel eyes met his. "Your cock inside me."

"*Fuck.*" He pressed his forehead to hers, trying not to come. "I'm not going to last long, Gemma."

"Oh?" She paused. "Because it's been a while for you?"

He met her gaze again. "It's been years. I haven't been with anyone since I left the military."

Her lips parted. "Why?"

"I never wanted anyone enough. And for a while there, I didn't want anyone to touch me."

In the firelight, he saw the flush on her cheeks. "But you want me."

More than he could ever express. "Yes."

"I want you inside me." She licked her lips. "And I

want to watch you while you're inside me. I want you to fuck me, enjoy me, and I want to watch when you come."

A hoarse expulsion of air escaped him. He slammed his palm against the wall to hold himself upright. "Gemma, I don't have any condoms."

She turned her head and bit his ear, then rubbed her sweet body against his. "It's okay. I have an IUD, and I'm healthy. I'm assuming you got a clean bill of health when you came home?"

"Yeah." Fuck her with nothing between them? Slide his cock inside her and feel every slick inch? He felt dizzy at the thought.

Her legs clenched at his sides. "Now, Boone. Take whatever you want."

BOONE MADE a raw sound that reverberated through Gemma. His face looked dark in the firelight, filled with need.

Had anyone ever wanted her as much as this man did?

A man who saw her—soft, curvy Gemma who liked to bake sweet things and put a smile on people's faces.

He saw her, he liked *her*. With Boone, she knew she was enough.

She felt his hand slide between their bodies, and he shoved his boxer shorts out of the way. Her chest hitched, her body throbbed. "Boone, hurry."

He shifted, and she felt the weight of his cock brush her skin. Her belly clenched.

Then, without any warning, he gripped her hip, then thrust home.

She made a sound, her legs tightening on him. He was only half inside her, and she felt the stretch.

Then his hot mouth was on hers. "So damn tight, Gemma. You can take me."

She wasn't in pain exactly, just discomfort as she adjusted to his size. Boone was inside her, filling her.

"*Deeper*," she murmured, clutching at him.

"Christ, Gemma, you feel so damn good."

"You feel good too. Hot and hard, filling me up."

He groaned. "I can't... I can't keep control when you talk like that."

She trailed her lips up the side of his neck and nibbled at his ear. "So don't keep control. Let go."

As she watched, she saw his control snap. He pinned her harder to the wall, thrusting all the way inside her.

She cried out, gripping him tightly. His thrusts were hard and fast, almost desperate. She moaned his name, loving the way he powered inside her. It wasn't cautious, there was no finesse. It was raw, hard, real.

"That's it, Gemma, baby. Take me." His voice was a low growl. "Take my cock."

Gemma couldn't do anything but hold on and moan. The sensations were building inside her. She felt a hand between them, and his thumb found her clit.

"Say my name," he demanded.

"*Boone*."

His thrusts got harder, more frantic. She felt owned, possessed, needed.

"I want to feel you come," he said.

"I'm close. *Please.*"

"God, not enough. I can't get close enough."

He kept filling her and stroking her clit. Everything inside her contracted, then exploded in a flash.

"*Boone—*" She lost the ability to talk and shook under the force of her orgasm. Her pussy clenched, and she heard him groan.

"Mine. This is all *mine.*" His next thrust was deep.

"Yes, yours." Her voice was breathless. She forced her eyes to stay open. She wanted to watch.

Then Boone threw his head back and made an animal sound. His body convulsed, and she saw the cords of his throat strain.

God, he was beautiful. The look on his face said exactly what he was feeling. Watching his pleasure was just as good as feeling her own.

She knew he was having the same explosive, knock-you-sideways climax that she'd had.

Finally, he slumped against her. Their bodies were both lax, and they were both breathing heavily.

"I was way too rough."

She snorted. "You were perfect. Newsflash. Some women like it hot, rough, and awesome."

He made a masculine sound, then lifted her away from the wall.

Gemma squeaked. "If I'm too heavy—"

"Be quiet. You're not heavy." He carried her to the couch and set her on her feet in front of the fire. "Don't move."

He disappeared into the bathroom.

She bit her lip. It was a little weird to stand there

wearing only a T-shirt, with Boone's come sliding down her thighs.

He returned with a cloth. He knelt in front of her, and she sucked in a breath. As he cleaned her, she looked down at his dark head.

Pure protector. He was meant to look out for others. He wasn't meant to be alone.

He rose. "Stay there."

He returned from the bedroom with blankets and pillows off the bed. He spread them out and made a makeshift bed in front of the fireplace.

Oh.

He sat and tugged her down. "Shirt off."

She hesitated. "I'll be naked."

"That's the point."

"I could get cold."

"I'll keep you warm." He pulled the shirt over her head.

"Um, it's not exactly being cold I'm worried about. I've curves and a few little rolls..."

"You're beautiful, Gemma. I love the firelight on your skin." He cupped one of her breasts. "And I'd be more than happy if you never, ever cover these."

She smiled. He made his adoration of her body clear. "Men. Give them boobs, and they're happy."

He smiled, looking so young. "We're simple creatures."

"You should be naked too," she said. "It's only fair."

In the way of men, he shucked his boxer shorts without a second thought.

God, that body of his...

ANNA HACKETT

He pushed her back on the blankets, his gaze on her. The fire cast dancing shadows over his face.

"What now?" she asked, breathless.

"Now, I get my mouth on that pussy of yours again. I've been dreaming about it."

"*Oh.*" She licked her lips. "Go ahead."

CHAPTER THIRTEEN

D amn, he loved the sounds Gemma made. Her body bowed as he licked her, then sucked her swollen clit. Her soft thighs clenched under his hands.

He looked up, savoring her naked body spread out for him in front of the fire.

"God, Boone, I'm going to—" On a cry, she came. Her body shook, and he kept sucking, loving the taste of her.

Pure sweetness. He'd never get enough of her.

His cock was hard again. Like he'd never come. He shifted, kneeling between her legs and nudging her thighs apart. Her breasts were rising and falling with her fast breaths.

"Boone."

Damn, the way she looked at him made him feel good, whole.

She pulled him down, and he covered her softness with his hardness.

Her mouth moved along his jaw. "Come inside me."

Boone was shaking with need. He didn't want to rush

this time around. Give her more than a hard and fast pounding against the wall.

He'd savor her. Cherish her. Show her how much he wanted her.

He notched the head of his cock between her legs. She was slick and warm. Their gazes met, and he slowly pushed inside her.

She moaned his name. Damn, she was so beautiful.

He took her hands in his and pressed them over her head. He moved inside her—slow and steady.

Her lips parted, and she never looked away. He'd never felt so connected to somebody else.

Pleasure swelled inside him. For a second, he closed his eyes, breathing through the sensation of feeling this woman. It was just the two of them—nothing but the feel and smell of Gemma.

He opened his eyes, needing to see her.

"So good," she panted. "So perfect."

"No, you're perfect." He pulled back and thrust back inside her. "So warm and tight." He leaned back, watching where his cock split her.

Damn. He moved his thumb to her clit and rubbed. She cried out his name.

"That's it, baby. Take it."

"Give me everything." Her body arched. "I want it all."

"Take my cock, Gemma. You look so good filled with me."

She moaned, her breasts heaving.

Boone gripped her hips, holding her tight as he powered inside her.

Her hands clutched at his shoulders, her nails biting into his skin. "Make us come, Boone. Together."

"*Yes*." His control was gone, his hips moving faster.

His. The word echoed in his brain. He wanted to keep her. The dark need ripped from his battered soul.

"Boone, oh, God. Hurry, I'm coming—"

On his next thrust, her pussy clenched tight on his cock. She screamed, her body shaking, her hands flexing on him.

He thrust home one last time. "*Gemma*."

"*Boone*."

The orgasm hit him like an electric shock. He made a guttural sound, the first hot jet of come almost hurting. Groaning her name, he could barely think through the pleasure. It felt like everything was pouring out of him.

Spent, he collapsed, catching himself and dropping down beside her. Instantly, she snuggled into him, a blissed-out expression on her face.

"I'm floating," she said dreamily.

He smiled. He felt like he was floating, too.

"Let's stay right here, forever," she said.

He ran a hand down her back. "Someone will need to put more wood on the fire and get food. And feed Atlas."

She jolted, looking around. "Oh, he wasn't watching, was he?"

"No. He's in the bedroom."

"Phew." She pressed a kiss to his chest. "I guess we both broke our droughts in the most spectacular way possible."

He stroked a hand down her side. "We did."

He felt a small sting of guilt. She was in a bad situation, dependent on him to keep her safe. He shouldn't have touched her.

"No, Boone Hendrix, no thinking."

He met her gaze. She looked ready to fight him.

"I'm a big girl who knows *exactly* what she wants." Her tone was fierce.

He smiled. "Okay."

She nodded. "Good." Then her voice lowered. "I want to kiss you."

"So kiss me."

She did, pressing her lips to his.

He slid a hand up into the tangle of her hair. "You can do anything you want to me."

Her eyes sparked. "Really?" She pushed him flat onto his back and climbed on top.

———

BOONE SIPPED HIS COFFEE, watching Gemma play with Atlas as she baked muffins in the kitchen.

There was a rap at the front door. "Morning."

Boone rose and let Shep in. "Morning."

"Sleep well?" his friend asked.

Boone knew Shep didn't miss much. He was eyeing Boone with a speculative look. Boone had tidied up their impromptu bed in front of the fireplace, but he was pretty sure Shep knew that Boone had spent the best part of the night with his arms wrapped around Gemma.

Hell, he'd spent most of the night inside Gemma.

"We did," Boone replied.

"Smells good in here."

"Gemma bakes. She's making muffins."

"You lucky fuck," Shep murmured. As he strolled in, Atlas woofed a greeting.

"She's also baking dog treats," Boone said.

Shep shook his head.

"Morning, Shep." Gemma's face was flushed, her hair in a messy bun. "Coffee?"

"Please."

"I'm guessing black."

"You guess right." Shep took the mug from her, then nodded at the door.

Boone got the message. "We'll be outside."

She smiled at him. "The muffins will be ready soon."

The Colorado sunlight seemed brighter than Vermont. Boone scanned the pretty yellow of the Aspen trees, mixed in amongst the evergreens. He breathed in the crisp mountain air.

"Haven't seen you this relaxed...ever," Shep said.

Boone shrugged a shoulder.

"It's because of her." Shep sipped his coffee. "You're falling for her."

Boone shifted, his gut tying in knots. "She's in danger. I had no right to touch her. I'm her protection."

"She isn't a job. You're more than just her body-guard." Shep's gaze met Boone's, his face serious. "You couldn't pay me to put up with a woman, but there's no doubt looking at you that you're fucking happy right now."

"Shit." Boone sipped his coffee and burned his tongue. "I don't want a relationship. I don't want the feelings. When you let people close..." It hurt when you fucking lost them.

Shep gripped his shoulder. "I know you lost your family, Boone. Your parents and your uncle. Then we lost Charlie, Julio, and Miles." Shep looked away and dragged in a breath. "None of them would want you to be unhappy."

"I couldn't save them."

"You are *not* to blame for their deaths, Boone. You barely made it out alive. When we got there, those fuckers were about to kill you."

Vander, Shep, and the others had arrived just in time. Sometimes, Boone wished they hadn't rescued him. That he'd died with his friends.

"They knew what they signed up for," Shep said. "We all did. They sure as hell wouldn't blame you."

Boone noted Shep didn't include himself in that little speech. He knew Shep struggled with it as well. The death of their friends was just the culmination of a long line of things that had eaten at them.

"The shit creeps up on you sometimes." Shep's jaw tightened. "It sucks we lost them. It sucks that I wasn't in time. It will always suck."

"I often wish it had been me." Boone dragged a hand through his hair. "That Julio was still here with his kids. Teaching Eddie to ride a fucking bike."

"I know you taught his kid to ride a bike."

"And I know you bought the bike for him."

All the Ghost Ops team members looked in on the families of Julio, Charlie, and Miles. Boone tried to get down to see Julio's kids a couple of times a year. He checked in on Charlie's widow, and had walked Miles' former fiancée down the aisle after she'd met a new guy. The night before the wedding, she'd cried on Boone's shoulder, still grieving for the man she'd lost.

"Their families will be looked after. Vander and the rest of the team make sure of it." Shep paused. "The guys would be pissed if you weren't enjoying life, living life, because of the guilt."

Boone sipped his coffee. He knew Shep wasn't wrong. But it was one thing to know something in your head, and another to believe it in your heart. "Then they'd be pissed at you. Hiding up here."

Shep growled. "I'm *not* hiding. I'm happy. I don't want people in my business constantly." He crossed his arms over his chest. "And this isn't about me. The guys would be *really* pissed if you let that beautiful woman who can fucking bake slip through your fingers."

"She's so...good, Shep. She's been through her own crap, but she's still sweet and light, smiles all the time."

"Grab onto that, Boone."

"I've got to keep her safe first."

"And I'll help you. Whatever you need."

"Boone?" Gemma's voice came from inside. "Can you tell Shep I'm cooking dinner tonight? As a thank you. Is there a particular meal he'd like—?"

"Spaghetti and meatballs," Shep said without hesitation.

Boone heard the sweet sound of Gemma's laugh. "Got it. And for dessert?"

"Apple pie."

"Then make sure you're hungry," she called out.

Shep set his empty mug down on the porch railing. "I'm going to work out. I have a gym set up at the end of the barn. Sounds like I'll need my appetite. You need anything?"

Boone shook his head. "You've already done so much."

"Save me some of those muffins too." Shep pointed a finger at him.

Boone smiled. "I'll see what I can do, but no promises."

"Asshole." But Shep was smiling as he strode off toward the barn.

Back inside, Boone heard Gemma singing to a rapt Atlas as she took trays out of the oven. She set the muffins to cool on the counter, then grabbed a dog biscuit, throwing it between her hands like a hot potato. Boone noted the damn things were shaped like bones.

"Ready?" She tossed it. Atlas leaped up and snatched it out of the air.

Gemma laughed and gave him a rigorous rub. "Clever boy."

She smelled good, looked good, felt good. Boone just stared at her. In that second, he knew he'd happily die for her. Anything to keep her safe and smiling.

Shep was right. Julio, Charlie, and Miles would want him to live. They'd kick his ass if he avoided whatever was going on between him and Gemma.

She looked up. "Muffins just need to cool. I'm thinking I'll make some cupcakes next."

Boone stalked over to her. He needed to kiss her. Desperately.

He hauled her into his arms and took her mouth with his.

As his tongue stroked hers, she made a gasping sound, her hands curling into his shirt. When he lifted his head, she had a dreamy look on her face.

"Boone?"

"Gemma."

She let out a happy sigh. "I have sex tingles."

It startled a laugh out of him. "I like the sound of that." He pushed a strand of her hair back behind her ear. "I'll help you make the cupcakes."

Her eyes widened. "Really?"

He squeezed her. "Really."

Then he kissed her again until she was clinging to him, her eyes closed and pink on her cheeks.

"You smell good enough to eat," he murmured.

That pink flush deepened.

"So, where do we start?"

She blinked. "Huh?"

"With the cupcakes."

"You're really going to help me?"

"Yes. Give me a second to let Atlas out to roam, and I'm all yours."

———

GEMMA FOCUSED INTENTLY on pouring the last of the cupcake mixture into the trays she'd found. Thank God Shep, or more likely whoever had built the cabins before he'd purchased the place, had stocked the kitchens with every gadget and item they could think of. She couldn't imagine Shep Barlow buying baking trays and spatulas.

"Open the oven for me, please?"

Boone opened the door. He looked far too good in the kitchen, but he made a surprisingly good baking partner.

She slid the tray in and wiped her hands on the towel tucked into her waistband. She let her gaze wander over the way his denim jeans hugged his ass. An ass she'd had her hands all over last night. A hot throb in her lower belly made her bite her lip.

As much as she wished she could pretend the world didn't exist, that it was just the two of them and Atlas in a beautiful cabin in the mountains, baking cupcakes and having spectacular sex, she knew she couldn't bury her head in the sand.

"After we finish the cupcakes, I want to look into Carruthers."

Boone's jaw tightened, but he gave a tight nod.

"We need to find what he's after. This isn't about ransom. He wants something and he thinks I can give it to him."

"We'll do some digging."

"Thanks." She set her shoulders back. "First, we need to prep some frosting. Cupcakes with no frosting are crime."

Beside her, Boone nabbed a muffin and bit into it. It was his fourth one. "What do you want me to do?"

"Grab the milk for me?"

Expertly, she pulled out a bowl and started putting in the ingredients. She added the milk that Boone handed her and started mixing.

"We'll get the frosting ready, and once the cupcakes are cooked and cooled, we'll ice them."

"Then eat them." He sounded like a little boy.

"Yes."

Gemma wanted to spoil this man. She didn't think he'd had enough fun in his life.

Well, today he was getting cupcakes with extra frosting. She kept mixing, lifted the wooden spoon, and turned.

And hit Boone in the face.

"*Oh.*" She bit her lip. "I'm sorry."

He had a streak of frosting on his nose.

"That's assault with a deadly weapon."

"I didn't mean it." Trying not to laugh, she swiped her finger along the spoon. Then she smeared frosting all over his stubbled cheek. "I meant that."

His eyes turned hooded. "Oh, you're in trouble now." He stepped forward, trapping her against the counter. Then he dipped a hand into the bowl of frosting, then smeared the sweet stickiness over her lips and down her jaw.

"Boone!" Her chest hitched. She saw the heat in his gaze.

He lowered his head, licking the frosting off her lips. Then his mouth ran over her jaw. She tipped her head back, her belly filled with fizzes of desire. His mouth traveled lower.

"*Boone...*" Now his name was just a moan.

He shoved her shirt up and smeared frosting over her belly. Then he dropped to his knees and licked it off her skin.

She cried out, instantly wet between her legs. But she'd wanted to spoil him, not the other way around.

She grabbed his shirt and urged him up. When he stood, she spun him so that his back was to the counter.

"My turn." She attacked the belt and got his jeans open.

"Gemma, fuck—"

She drew his cock out. It looked like the rest of him, long and hard. She stroked him, enjoying his low groan. Then she dipped her finger in the frosting. His hot, golden gaze was on her like a laser as she licked her finger. His lips parted.

Then she ran her finger over the swollen head of his cock. His body bucked.

Oh, it was intoxicating to have this power over him. To know she affected him as much as he affected her.

Then she slowly lowered to her knees.

She looked up at him and then licked the head of his cock. His groan was long and loud. She sucked him into her mouth.

"*Gemma.*" The word was garbled, and his hands clenched in her hair. He tugged her closer.

She took him deeper. She took her time sucking him, listening to his groans. She bobbed her head.

"I don't want to come in your pretty mouth." His voice sounded like grit. He yanked her up, and in two seconds, he had her leggings and panties gone. He lifted her onto the counter.

Then he moved his big body between her legs, fitting his cock to where she was wet and achy. He surged forward and was deep inside her in one thrust.

"*Boone*." So good. So full.

He started to drive into her, and she gripped the edge of the counter. It was wild, filled with need.

"Jesus, I could stay here forever." His gold eyes held hers.

For a second, she wanted to look away. She felt like he could see inside her—to every dark corner.

"You fill me up." She reached down, touching where his girth stretched her to the limit.

"Hang on, Gemma." He picked up speed. Every thrust wrenched more cries from her. The next few minutes blurred—it was a hot, sexy assault on the senses.

She gripped him tighter, her heels digging into his ass. She heard something get knocked off the counter and hit the floor, but she didn't care.

Shockingly, her climax hit without warning. She screamed his name.

He pounded into her a few more times, then planted deep, and let out a low, tortured groan. She felt his hot release inside her.

God. Gemma felt wrecked, in the best possible way. She clutched at him to stay upright.

"Gemma. Jesus." He kissed her.

When they finally separated, she saw the upturned bowl of frosting on the floor. There was sticky, sugary deliciousness everywhere.

"We'll need to make more frosting," she said, deadpan.

The sound of his low laugh made her grin.

CHAPTER FOURTEEN

"Okay, so Carruthers is a wealthy businessman who lives in London." Gemma sat cross-legged on the floor, her hair up in a messy knot, and the laptop on the coffee table in front of her. Her fingers flew over the keyboard.

Boone sat behind her on the couch and finished another cupcake. It was his third one, and that was after he'd eaten four muffins earlier. She loved watching his obvious enjoyment of her food. "You like my cupcakes?"

"Best damn thing I've ever eaten." The corner of his lips lifted. "Except for you."

She felt heat in her cheeks and had to force herself to focus back on her search.

"You might prefer baking, but it looks like you know your way around a computer."

"The computer science degree comes in handy sometimes. Now, let's dig a little deeper on Mr. Carruthers." She made a humming sound. "I have to say, this machine and the secure connection are excellent. Darcy knows her stuff."

"Carruthers has legitimate businesses, right?" Boone asked.

"Yes. Manufacturing, refrigeration, and air conditioning." She frowned. "Probably makes it easy to hide nefarious deals in industrial warehouses."

"Nefarious?" Boone smiled at her.

"It means evil, Boone."

"I know. I've just never heard someone actually use it."

She poked her tongue out at him. "Oh, Darcy also sent through some data on Carruthers that she'd collated." Gemma clicked the keys, then she sucked in a harsh breath.

"Gemma?" He pressed a hand to her shoulder.

"It's a list of the arms sales he's allegedly made. *God.* Missiles. Material for bombs." She felt sick. "He sells to terrorist groups, Boone."

"Yeah, I know."

"You don't look surprised."

He shrugged. "I unfortunately came across some shitty people over my years with Ghost Ops. The worst were the ones who put on a good-guy front to the world, while they did the complete opposite in the shadows."

Gemma whirled onto her knees. "Groups like the Taliban. The people who attack our troops, who took you and killed..."

"My friends. Yeah, men like Carruthers are scum."

She leaned against his leg for a second, offering him

comfort, then swiveled back to the laptop. "Do you think we can find what Carruthers is shopping around for? Maybe that'll help me work out why he's coming after me? Do arms dealers have a shopping list or a menu?"

"Vander could get that information."

"I'll send him an email." She hunched over the laptop, then sent off the email. "Now, we just wait."

"Yes."

"Waiting is no fun."

"We can agree on that."

Gemma rose. "I'm going to get started on dinner. I promised Shep an excellent meal and I'm going to deliver. First up, I have a pie to bake."

Baking and cooking kept her busy, and kept her mind off the arms dealer hunting her. She lost herself in the pleasure of making the apple pie and getting the crust just right. She made meatballs, and prepped her famous garlic bread.

As dinner time neared, she darted around the kitchen. She wanted the meal to be perfect. As a thank you to Boone and Shep for everything they were doing to help her.

The men were currently out on the porch, drinking a beer and throwing a stick to Atlas. The cool afternoon had given way to a cold evening. The temperatures had dropped, and Boone had the fire roaring.

Smiling, she checked on the spaghetti she had boiling on the stove. She'd doubled the portion she usually made —she was pretty sure Boone and Shep would eat a lot more than she was used to.

The apple pie sat on a plate on the counter. She smiled. She was sure Shep would love it.

She wished they were all just friends, sharing a meal.

She wished she wasn't being hunted.

Gemma sagged against the counter, her mind turning to Carruthers. Who the hell did he think he was? Ordering men to snatch her? And why?

She sighed. Thanks to her father, she'd met lots of powerful, wealthy men who believed they could do whatever the hell they wanted.

Hands touched her shoulders, and she jumped.

"Take it easy." Boone was looking at her, worry on his face. She hadn't even heard him come inside.

"Sorry, I was daydreaming."

He tipped her chin up. "You mean worrying."

She blew out a breath. "It's kind of hard not to."

He smoothed her hair back behind her ear. "You're not alone, Gemma."

"I know."

"Smells good in here." Shep walked past them and opened the fridge. He pulled out another bottle of beer. "Is it time to eat?"

Gemma smiled. "Yes, it is. You two sit down and I'll serve up."

Soon, she had the garlic bread and salad she'd made in the center of the table. She served the men large plates of meatballs, and a smaller one for herself.

Atlas hovered nearby, but she knew Boone had already fed him. She slipped him a dog treat and his tail wagged.

"Wow." Shep stared at the plate of food hungrily. "If this tastes half as good as it looks and smells..."

She beamed at him. "It does. But make sure you leave room for apple pie."

"Oh, there'll be room." Shep dug in.

Boone gave her a small smile before he started his own meal.

"Fuck," Shep said. "Gemma, this is *good*."

She felt a flush in her cheeks. It was one of her most favorite things in the world when people enjoyed her food. "Thanks."

"No, thank you. It's been a long time since I've had a good home-cooked meal that I haven't thrown together myself." He ate another large forkful of food.

It was after they'd eaten, and after Boone and Shep—despite her protests that she could help—had cleaned up the table and kitchen, that she found herself on the couch in front of the fire. She snuggled into Boone's side, Atlas lying at their feet. Shep sat in an armchair across from them.

The men had switched to Scotch, both of them cradling glasses.

"So, any more information on this Carruthers?" Shep asked.

Gemma stiffened, and Boone stroked a hand down her arm.

"Not yet," Boone said. "He's rich and British, that's all we have."

"And he's an arms dealer." Shep's tone said exactly what he thought about that. He sipped his drink.

"How does the man sleep at night?" Gemma asked

quietly. "When you're responsible for so much death and suffering."

"He probably doesn't feel anything," Shep said. "Doesn't care."

"Or he justifies it to himself," Boone said. "That he's not the one pulling the trigger or detonating the bomb. That the weapons he sells aren't the problem. It's the people who use them."

"Right, but he sells dangerous weapons to dangerous people. And profits off it." She shook her head. "I'll never understand."

Boone gently tugged on her hair. "Try to turn it off for a bit. You're just a woman relaxing in a cabin in the Rocky Mountains."

She wrinkled her nose. "It's not that easy."

He lowered his voice. "I'll help you relax later."

She shivered, desire a lazy coil in her belly. Oh, yes, despite everything they'd done to each other last night and today, she wanted more. So much more.

"Miles loved a good Scotch." Shep was studying his glass.

Against her, Gemma felt Boone stiffen. She pressed a hand to his chest.

"Remember that expensive bottle of..." Shep shook his head. "I can't remember the name of it. The bottle he wanted when he got engaged."

Boone's lips twitched. "I remember. The whole team pitched in to buy it for him. Damn stuff tasted like ash."

Shep laughed. It was a low, sexy rumble that Gemma guessed he didn't use very much.

She stayed quiet and listened as they reminisced about their fallen friends.

Shep leaned forward. "Remember the time Julio drank that entire bottle of tequila? He was celebrating when Martina had Eddie."

"Eddie is Julio's son," Boone told Gemma. "He was sad that he missed the birth while we were away on a mission, but he sure made up for it with the enthusiasm of his celebration."

"Never seen anyone puke so much." Shep grunted. "He was green the next day on the helo."

Gemma smiled. She wondered if they let themselves remember their friends—and the good times—very often. "What was Charlie's drink of choice?"

Shep groaned. "Craft beer. He used to brew his own."

Boone chuckled. "He was obsessed. Talked about his home-brewing *all* the time."

"Finally, we were all stateside, and he made us try it." Shep pulled a face.

"He called it Ghost Hops." Boone started laughing even harder.

"Fuck, I'd forgotten that." Shep's deep laugh joined Boone's.

"It tasted horrible," Boone told her.

Shep snorted. "It tasted like dirty bath water."

"It sounds like they were good friends, and lots of fun."

Boone toyed with her hair. "They were." There was a ding from Boone's pocket. "That's my phone." He pulled it out and looked at the screen, his brow furrowing.

"There's a message from Vander."

Gemma couldn't help but stiffen, her good mood leaking away.

Boone's face hardened and he met her gaze. "Ace found something on the dark web. He's sent it through."

Mouth dry, she reached for the laptop sitting closed on the coffee table. She opened it and peered at the screen. "Oh, God. Apparently, Carruthers is planning an auction very soon."

A muscle ticked in Boone's jaw. "Of what?"

"An encrypted satellite targeting system called Flux."

He frowned. "Okay."

She kept reading the information, her chest winding tighter. "Boone, Flux is used by countries across the world. Militaries across the world. They use this satellite targeting system for their missiles and drones."

"Fuck," Shep muttered.

Boone looked like he'd been hit hard. "So, if someone had their hands on Flux, they could hack our military's missile strikes, drone missions...?"

She nodded, horror filling her. "And not just our military, but most of our allies as well."

"Are you a secret expert in satellite targeting systems?" Shep asked.

"No." She tapped on the keyboard. "Let me look into Flux a bit more. It was designed by a tech company called ZonaTech..."

Oh, God. An icy cold washed over her.

"What is it?" Boone asked.

She swallowed, her throat tight. "I did work with

ZonaTech. When I was at Expanse. I was the project lead."

He leaned forward. "What was the project, Gemma?"

She swallowed again. "Data storage for low-orbit communications satellites. We did lots of behind-the-scenes systems stuff."

"Systems that ZonaTech then probably used when they created Flux for military applications," Shep said.

Boone nodded. "Carruthers thinks that you can give him a backdoor into Flux."

"Which he then wants to sell off to the highest bidder." She pressed a hand to her stomach. "I feel sick."

"Send the intel to Vander."

She nodded and saw Shep and Boone lock gazes.

"It isn't just Gemma's safety at risk now," Boone said quietly, "but national security. Hell, global security. If terrorists or unfriendly nations could redirect other countries' missiles and drones..."

"How could someone do this?" Gemma shot to her feet. "Carruthers must have no conscience."

Boone rose and wrapped his arms around her. "Like a lot of people, he just cares more about money and power."

She looked up at him. "You don't?"

His gaze locked on hers. "I have more than enough money. I don't need much. And I don't give a flying fuck about power." For a second, his gaze changed, and she knew he'd gone somewhere dark. "In life-or-death situations, it doesn't matter much."

"You haven't once asked about my father, or—"

Boone gripped her jaw. "Because what I feel for you has nothing to do with your father."

God, this man. She managed a small smile. "You don't want a job at Expanse?"

"Fuck, no."

"Or a Ferrari and a few million dollars?"

He shook his head. "I'm a truck man, and I don't need a few million dollars."

"You really mean that," she murmured.

"Yes." He nibbled her lips. "Now, more of your sweet body, and lots of your cupcakes, those I want."

"I'll take a Ferrari," Shep said.

She jerked. She'd forgotten the other man was there. Shep headed for the door.

"My cue to leave. Thanks for dinner, Gemma. I'll see you two in the morning." Then he was gone.

Gemma wound her arms around Boone, and he pulled her close. Right here, she felt safe. Like nothing could touch her.

"Boone, Flux is worth a lot to Carruthers. He's not gonna stop coming after me."

Boone's grip tightened. "Carruthers is not touching you, Gemma. I swear."

———

BOONE EYED the mine structure high on the hill above them. It was a dilapidated wooden building clinging to the hillside. Below it was a patch of yellow aspens surrounded by dense evergreen trees.

He was sitting on the porch, watching Gemma and Atlas run around on the grass.

He hadn't had a nightmare last night. He'd spent the night spooning Gemma, or fucking her, and the rest of the time, he'd slept like a log.

Then he'd started his day with his head between her legs, after which they'd had a very long shower.

Despite everything going on, he hadn't felt this light in a long time.

Must be the good food, cupcakes, and hot sex.

No, that wasn't the truth. It was Gemma.

She'd woken him up.

And she was in more danger than he'd thought. His hand clenched into a fist. Whatever he had to do to keep her safe, he'd do it.

The rumble of Shep's truck caught his ear. His friend had left earlier this morning to head into the local town for some things.

Shep parked, then sliced out of the truck, and Boone stiffened. He knew his friend well enough to tell he was tense and worried about something.

Shep headed over, watching as Atlas leaped on Gemma. She went down, giggling as she play-wrestled with Boone's dog.

Damn, watching the pair of them made his chest tighten.

Shep leaned against the porch railing.

"I'm guessing the trip to town didn't run smoothly?" Boone said.

"There are some guys in town. Asking questions. I

couldn't risk getting too close, but I reckon they're your mercenaries."

"Fucking hell." Boone bit off a curse. "Shep, how the hell could they have found her? They've managed to track her—" He broke off, horror dawning.

Shep cursed. "They have a tracker on her."

"She has new clothes—"

"It has to be on her body somewhere."

Fuck. Boone rose. Another violation of Gemma's life. "If they have a tracker, why are they asking questions in town? Why aren't they here already?"

Shep's mouth flattened. "Reception sucks here. Maybe they can't get an exact lock on her, just a general area."

They didn't have a lock on her yet, but he knew the clock was ticking.

He looked up and saw Gemma watching him. Her smile was gone, and her face was pale. Slowly, she walked over.

"What's going on?"

"Shep saw some of the mercs in town."

Her mouth dropped open. "You're kidding. How are they here?"

Boone walked down the steps and cupped her face. "We'll take care of it."

"How do they keep finding me?" There was an edge to her voice.

She'd already coped with so much. He wouldn't let her break. "We think they put a tracker on you."

Her eyes went wide, her freckles stark on her cheeks.

"A tracker? But I'm wearing different clothes, and we have clean phones."

"Do you have a scratch or cut that you didn't have before your abduction?"

"Yes. You know I do. I got banged up escaping—" She sucked in a sharp breath. "They put a tracker inside me. In my *body*." A wild look crossed her face, and she shook her head. "*No*. God, no."

"Gemma, it's okay—"

Her fingers gripped his forearms, nails biting in. "Get it out, Boone. Please. *Now*."

"Okay. Okay." He looked at Shep. "Take care of Atlas for a minute."

Shep nodded. "There's a first aid kit in the bathroom."

As Boone led Gemma into the cabin, his dog barged forward to follow.

"Atlas, go with Shep."

Atlas ignored him and pressed against Gemma's legs.

Boone sighed. "Fine. Come on."

He led her to the bathroom, and Atlas followed.

"Let me check your scalp and hair first." He worked his fingers through the silky strands. She was biting her lip.

"I'll check your healing wounds next."

She nodded.

"It'll be best if you take your clothes off."

She wrinkled her nose and shoved her leggings down. "This is an unfun reason to get naked." Her sweater and shirt followed. It left her wearing a simple black bra and panties, but his body still responded regardless.

She held out an arm, and he gently probed the scratches. There was nothing that he could feel. He checked her feet and up her slim legs.

"I have a scratch on the back of my neck? But I got that after I escaped from them."

Boone stood behind her and pushed her hair aside. He checked the still-healing wound, but didn't find a tracker.

He met her gaze in the mirror and saw the sheen of tears in her eyes. They killed him. "So brave."

She sniffed. "I don't feel brave."

"Any other scratches that are bothering you? That are itchy? Swollen?"

Her brow wrinkled. "I don't think—" She gasped. "*Wait*. My hip." She shoved her panties half down.

Boone ignored the sweet curve of her belly the best he could. His gaze locked on the ugly scratch by her left hipbone.

"I thought it was just a little infected."

He gently probed and felt a lump.

She made a sound. "It's there. I can tell from your face."

He nodded. "I need to cut it out."

"Do it."

"I don't have any anesthetic. It'll hurt."

Her chin lifted. "I don't care. I just want it out."

He gripped her hips, then lifted her onto the vanity. He pulled out the first aid kit. Inside, he found a scalpel and some antiseptic wipes. He disinfected the blade, then swiped a fresh wipe over her hip. He lifted the knife. Beside him, Atlas growled.

"I know, boy. I don't want to hurt her."

Gemma touched the side of Boone's head. "But you need to, so you can keep me safe." Her other hand reached down and gripped Atlas at the back of his neck. "Do it."

"Baby, I don't want you in pain." He felt like his chest was filled with bricks.

She leaned forward and kissed him. "I need you, Boone. Get that thing out of me."

Nodding, he gritted his teeth. Then he pressed the scalpel to her skin and started to cut.

She hissed. He kept cutting, and a tear rolled down her cheek. Atlas made an unhappy sound.

It felt like an eternity, but finally, the cut was wide enough. Boone set the bloody scalpel down in the sink, and picked up some tweezers, quickly giving them a wipe, as well. Bracing himself, he dug into the wound.

She made a low sound.

"Almost there, baby."

She nodded. "I'm okay. Keep going."

Damn, she was trying to reassure him. Finally, he clasped the tracker and pulled it out. "It's done."

He dropped the tiny cylinder into the sink, and it clinked against the porcelain. Then he rammed his fist down on the tracker. It crunched.

Breathing heavily, Gemma sagged. "Thank you."

He grabbed some gauze and dabbed her cut to wipe up the blood. Next, he pulled out antiseptic cream, medical glue, and a bandage from the first aid kit. He'd made the cut as small as he possibly could to keep the wound minimal. He cleaned it up, glued it shut, and carefully bandaged it.

Then he turned and hauled her into his arms, then dropped to his knees on the floor, rocking a little.

"I'm okay now." She clung to him. "Thank you."

He held her tightly.

Atlas added his weight, leaning into them.

Gemma gave a watery laugh. "You Hendrix men sure know how to take care of a girl."

CHAPTER FIFTEEN

"Gemma, fuck, don't stop."

She lifted her hips, her hands planted on Boone's chest. Then she rocked down, taking his cock deep inside her.

She moaned. She felt her orgasm building—big, a little scary, threatening to tear her apart.

"Get there, Gemma."

"*Boone.*" As she moaned his name, her fingers flexed on his chest. She rocked her hips faster, barely able to breathe.

His big cock filled her so well. She reached down and touched where he was buried inside her. His hand joined hers, stroking, and he found her clit.

Her release hit hard, and she screamed.

"That's it." He thrust his hips up. "I need that. Your tight pussy, your orgasm."

"They're yours." Her vision blurred.

Boone surged up and Gemma found herself flat on

her back. His powerful thrusts rocked the bed as he powered inside her.

Then he grunted and lodged his cock to the root. She felt his big body shudder as he poured himself inside her.

Perfection.

He rolled them so he was on his back, and she was on top of him.

She snuggled in, riding out the bliss of her post-orgasm goodness. He stroked a hand down her back, and she heard him breathe deep. She realized he was smelling her hair and smiled.

Suddenly, the bedroom door clicked open and Atlas bounded in. The dog jumped on the bed.

Gemma gasped and pulled at the sheets. "We're naked!"

"He's a dog. He doesn't care."

"I care." She wrapped the sheet around herself. Atlas flopped against her, and she couldn't help but smile.

When she looked up, Boone was grinning at her.

God. She wanted to see him smile like that every day. She also wanted naked sexy times every day as well.

Her stomach knotted. Aside from the fact that she was being hunted, she also lived in LA. He lived in Vermont. Alone with his dog, because she realized that he needed that. The simplicity and serenity.

Her finger moved over her hip, touching the bandage Boone had placed over the cut when he'd cut the tracker out this morning. The tracker was gone, but she knew the mercenaries were still out there. Somewhere.

"Boone." Shep's voice echoed from the front of the cabin. Next came the rap of a heavy fist on the front door.

Boone leaped out of the bed. "Something's wrong." He yanked on his jeans. "Get dressed." He snatched up a flannel shirt and stalked out of the bedroom.

One minute he'd been a relaxed, sexy man, the next, a focused soldier.

Gemma quickly dressed and hurried out. She found both Shep and Boone looking grim. "What's happening?"

"We have company." Shep jerked his head toward the front door. "Follow me. Grab your coats."

Worry eating at her, Gemma snatched up her coat and slipped it on. Boone stopped her and cupped her jaw.

"Whatever happens, I'll keep you safe."

She knew he meant it. He was an honorable, protective man to the core. She realized just how much she trusted him. She trusted very few people to be there for her, no questions asked, one hundred percent.

She took his hand and followed him out. Shep led them over to the barn.

The building wasn't exactly falling down, but it was old and worn. They went through the open door, and the inside was dark, dusty, and filled with cobwebs.

Shep led them past a rusted old truck and some other gear stacked around. She thought they might be bits of farm equipment, but she wasn't sure. In the back room, he shoved an old table aside and pushed back some boxes.

There was a trapdoor set in the floor.

He opened it, then descended a short ladder.

"Atlas, jump," Boone said.

The dog obeyed instantly.

Then Boone gestured for Gemma to go next.

Gripping the rungs, she carefully climbed down. The small space below was awash in blue light. She heard the clank of the trap door closing, then Boone followed her down.

She looked around and gasped.

There were six large computer screens on the wall. Shep sat in a chair in front of them.

All the screens showed video feed. Gemma squinted. Most of them displayed trees, and a few dirt roads.

On one, a dark truck was driving slowly down a road. On another, several black-clad figures moved stealthily through the trees.

"You're a paranoid bastard," Boone said.

"And it's lucky that I am. We have four teams moving in from different locations. They tripped my sensors."

"*God.*" She pressed a hand to her stomach.

"They must have gotten a hit off the tracker before I destroyed it," Boone said.

Gemma made a sound. This was all her fault. Boone pulled her close, his strong arms tight around her.

"Can we leave?" she asked. "Just drive away?"

Shep shook his head. "There's another team parked at the end of my driveway. We could go through the trees and hope to avoid the other teams who are converging."

"But these guys are good," Boone said.

Shep nodded.

"We need to hide Gemma, and make a stand." Boone's face sharpened. "End this, once and for all."

Make a stand? "You're going to fight them?"

Boone nodded.

Oh no. Her stomach dropped. "There are at least a dozen of them."

"I'm in," Shep said.

Boone swiveled her to look at him. "Gemma, you need to stay here. Whatever you hear, whatever happens, you can't come out."

Shep nodded. "Stay in here and stay quiet."

"Wait." Boone leaned forward. "Shep, zoom in on the truck."

His friend tapped the keyboard. Then both men cursed.

"What?" she demanded.

Boone's face looked the grimmest she'd ever seen. "They have RPGs."

Her eyes widened. "Missiles?"

"They could raze all the buildings to the ground," Shep said.

Her hand clenched on Boone's arm. "Oh, my God."

Boone squeezed the back of her neck. "We need to hide her somewhere safe."

"I know a place." Shep rose. "The mine."

THEY MOVED through the trees quickly, heading up the hillside toward the old mine. Atlas kept pace with Shep, who was leading the way.

"Boone—"

"It's going to be okay, Gemma."

But he and Shep were heavily outnumbered. He'd put in a call to Declan at Treasure Hunter Security for help, but Dec and his team were hours away. He carried a rifle and several weapons from Shep's stash.

The mercs were coming for Gemma. They didn't have much time.

All he had to do was keep them away from her. Make sure they couldn't find her.

He already knew he was falling for her. Hell, had fallen—body, heart, and soul.

Gemma Newhouse was his to protect, his to care for, his to love.

His to die for.

"The mine is a maze of old tunnels," Shep said. "Some are unsafe, so don't wander around. We'll find you a good area where you can hide."

Face pale, she nodded.

They reached a locked metal door set in the side of the mountain. Shep pulled a ring of keys out.

"We aren't going in through the mine building?" Boone eyed it farther up the hillside.

"The mercenaries might check there, or target it. This is a secondary adit. It's better hidden." Shep pushed the door open, and the hinges screeched in protest.

Boone clicked on a flashlight, as did Shep.

The tunnel wasn't large, but it looked sturdy enough. They kept together as they headed in.

"Keep taking the left-hand tunnels," Shep said.

They took the next left, then another. The next tunnel went straight into the mountainside. In a few areas, the tunnel widened up, and Boone saw old gear still stored there. There were stacked wooden crates, some old tools, and some rusted metal containers.

They reached an area where several tunnels speared off into the mountain. There were more wooden crates.

"This is a good spot," Shep said. "That larger tunnel leads up into the main mine building."

So Gemma wouldn't be trapped if someone made it this far.

Shep met Boone's gaze. "We need to get back and prepare."

For the incoming assault. Boone really wished they had their full Ghost Ops team to help. He turned to Gemma. She was scared, but holding it together.

"Here." He handed her the flashlight. "Stay hidden and quiet."

She nodded.

"And take this." He held out a handgun from Shep's supply. "I know you can use it."

She took the Smith & Wesson and looked at the rocky ground. So many emotions crossed her face.

"I'm also leaving Atlas with you."

She looked up now. "You'll be careful?"

"I'll do whatever I have to do to keep you safe."

Her face crumpled. "Boone—"

Then she threw her arms around him. He caught her, and her mouth slammed against his.

It was a hungry kiss, filled with emotion. She cupped his face. "You stay safe, Boone Hendrix. I want this to be over, and after this, you and I..."

"I know."

"I've been uncertain and unsure about the direction of my life for a long time. Trying to live up to other people's expectations. Trying to work out my own." She pressed her forehead to his. "You see me."

He held her tighter. "I do."

"And I see you. All of you. I want you, Boone. It's the surest thing I've ever known. Come back to me."

Damn. Things twisted inside him. Now he kissed her.

"Boone, we have to go," Shep said.

He forced himself to pull his lips from hers. Nodding, he set her down, then touched her cheek.

"Stay safe," she whispered fiercely.

He nodded. Then he knelt down and hugged his dog. "You stay with her, Atlas."

The dog butted his head against Boone's chest.

He stroked Atlas' muzzle. "I'll be back."

Then he made himself turn and walk away.

His jaw was tight as he trudged back down the tunnel. He didn't let himself look back at them. He had to get his mind off Gemma and focus on the mission.

"You okay?" Shep asked as they took another turn in the tunnel.

"I will be once we take down these assholes. Once I know she's safe."

"You are so fucked. She's got her hooks in you deep."

He glanced at his friend as they stepped out of the mine tunnel. "Yes. And I like it."

Shep shook his head and hefted his rifle. "Let's go and teach these assholes they shouldn't mess with Ghost Ops."

Boone smiled darkly. "Hell, yeah."

"I've got a couple of blinds set up in the trees around the cabins."

"Of course, you do."

"And we have just enough time to set up a few little surprises as well." Shep's lips curled. "If they think they have the advantage, they're in for a surprise."

Moving swiftly, they reached the cabins in a fraction of the time it took them to go up the hill with Gemma. Boone scanned the area.

Shep checked his camera feed on his phone. "They're getting close. We don't have much time. Come on."

Boone followed Shep back into the barn. His friend moved right to the back and stopped at a dusty crate. He flicked open the lid to uncover a tough metal container protected by a high-tech lock.

Shep pressed his palm to the lock, and it beeped. The lid opened with a hiss. Inside was a bunch of weapons and grenades nestled in foam.

"You turning into a doomsday prepper, Barlow?"

"Fuck you, Hendrix. You'll be thankful I have all this in a few minutes." He pulled out a ballistic vest and shoved it at Boone's chest.

They both pulled their vests on, tightening the fastenings. As Shep reached for the weapons, Boone grabbed his friend's arm. "Shep, thank you."

"Told you that you never, ever have to thank me for having your back."

Boone nodded. "Ditto."

They both grabbed more weapons and grenades. Then they hurried outside to set some boobytraps.

"I'll take the high blind," Shep said.

That made sense. Shep was a hell of a sniper.

"The other one's in that tree." He pointed. "Climb about halfway up and you'll spot it."

Boone couldn't see it, but he'd find it.

Shep nodded. "Let's do this." He fished something out of his pocket and held it out. Boone took the earpiece and slipped it in.

Then they clasped hands. "Good hunting, Shep. I'm glad you have my back."

"Always." Then the big man jogged into the trees.

Boone headed to the tree Shep had shown him, and climbed the branches. The blind was a small wooden platform hidden by camouflage netting. It blended perfectly into the branches and leaves. He got settled and checked his rifle.

"We'll pick off as many as we can," Boone said. "Then go hunting."

Once the mercenaries had his and Shep's locations, they'd need to switch to close-quarter combat.

"Acknowledged."

Boone glanced up at the mine. "Stay hidden and safe, Gemma."

Now it was time for him to protect his woman.

CHAPTER SIXTEEN

Boone lay flat and still, his eye pressed to the scope. He scanned the treeline beyond the cabins for movement.

Nothing yet.

His chest was tight, his gut churning. He was very aware that Gemma was up in the mine, alone except for Atlas. He hated that she was unprotected.

Usually on a mission he found his center, his mind cool and sharp. But with her so close, and a damn army coming for her, it made it hard.

She mattered too much.

So get your head in the game, Hendrix. Take these assholes down and protect her.

When he'd left her, she'd looked at him with trust. He wouldn't let her down. At the thought, his system steadied.

He pulled in a deep breath, then released it slowly.

"Bogeys incoming." Shep's steady voice came through the earpiece. "To the east."

Boone swiveled the rifle and saw them. Three men moving slowly, rifles in hand. "I've got them. They're mine."

"Got three more to the north," Shep added. "The other two teams can't be far away."

It was go time.

"Take out the targets on my mark," Boone murmured. He took aim. "*Mark.*"

He pulled the trigger. He saw the merc's head snap back. A second later, he heard the crack of his shot, and Shep's as well, echo through the trees. Boone seamlessly swiveled and aimed at a second merc. The man went down as well, before he could comprehend what was happening.

Boone fired on the third merc, but he was already diving for cover. The man's body jerked, so he'd been hit. But as he crawled out of sight, Boone knew it wasn't enough to take him out.

"Two down. I clipped the third guy. I'm not sure he's down."

"All mine are down," Shep confirmed.

Suddenly, bullets sprayed the tree.

Fuck. Boone flattened against the platform. The other teams had arrived.

He pulled back. "I'm taking fire."

"Time to move. The other two teams have joined the party."

Boone quickly dropped down through the branches. His boots hit the ground and he crouched, then headed into the trees.

"Shep, I'll take the team to the south."

179

"Acknowledged. I've got the others."

Boone's body knew its training. He moved silently through the trees. Just like the ghost his team had been named for. When his Ghost Ops team had been deployed on missions, there had been times they'd laid in wait, not moving for hours. People had walked right by them and never spotted them in their hiding places.

"Come out with the girl," a man shouted.

That's it, asshole, give me your location. He noted the Romanian accent. It was Radu. Boone slowed. Clearly the bullet Boone had put in the guy's shoulder in Denver hadn't slowed him down.

"Give her to us and we'll let you live."

Boone gave a mental snort. Sure, he was totally buying that. He crept in closer, his rifle up and ready. He noted movement off to his right, by the cabins. He saw a big merc moving closer. The guy had to be six foot six.

Boone needed to take him out first. He swung his rifle onto his shoulder, then darted through the trees. He paused and peeked through some foliage.

The merc was looking through the window of an empty cabin.

Across the clearing, he saw three other mercenaries fanning out. They'd come in force to get Gemma.

Behind the men, a big shape darted from the trees. Shep, Ka-Bar knife in hand, took one merc down silently. He dropped the body to the ground, then dissolved back into the trees.

"Oscar's down!" Another merc rushed to help his fallen friend.

The third merc frowned. "Grivas and Dale aren't answering comms."

"Find these fuckers!" Radu yelled from nearby.

Boom.

A small explosion rocked the clearing. Boone crouched lower and smiled. Someone had set off one of Shep's booby-traps. A cloud of smoke blew through the clearing.

Boone heard shouts, but he quickly moved in behind the cabins. He saw the big merc with his back to him.

Boone attacked. He wrapped his arms around the man's neck, and caught him in a chokehold. Boone used his body weight to pull them both backward, putting pressure on the man's throat and cutting off his air.

The guy struggled, and he was strong. Boone gritted his teeth and held tight.

The man rammed an elbow into Boone's thigh.

Fuck. Pain shot down his leg, but he ground his teeth together and pulled harder. He wasn't letting go. Finally, he felt the guy's body go lax, and lowered him to the ground. Quickly, Boone pulled zip-ties from his pocket and bound the man.

"You've signed your death warrants." Radu's raised voice echoed through the clearing. "We will kill you all. Slowly and painfully."

"Someone's pissed," Shep said dryly. "I'm coming your way."

"Acknowledged." Boone tried to see through the smoke hanging in the clearing from the explosion. How many mercs were left?

He pressed his back to the wall of another cabin and peered around.

Bullets hit the wood inches from his face, and he quickly ducked back.

"There's one of them! By the cabins."

Moving fast, Boone changed directions and darted between two other cabins.

"Where did he go?" a merc yelled.

"They're like fucking ghosts. There must be at least six of them."

Boone smiled.

"Get the thermal camera out," Radu ordered.

Shit. That wiped Boone's smile away. That would put him and Shep at a big disadvantage.

A second later, Shep appeared and crouched beside Boone.

"Still a few left," his friend said.

"Yeah. We need a plan fast, before they get that thermal camera up and running."

"Agreed." Shep looked around the corner of the cabin and stiffened. "Oh, shit."

Boone leaned around...

And spotted a merc aiming an RPG launcher toward the cabins.

"Fuck. *Run.*"

Shep and Boone sprinted for the trees.

Behind them, he heard the distinctive sound of the RPG firing.

Boom.

One of the cabins exploded in flames.

CROUCHED ON THE ROCKY GROUND, with only the faint illumination from her flashlight to help her see, Gemma stroked Atlas' side.

Waiting was horrible. Her brain was doing its best to come up with the worst possible scenarios.

"God," she said shakily.

Boone and Shep were out there, fighting to protect her. They were risking themselves for her.

Sensing her anxiety, Atlas rose and pressed against her. She buried her face in his fur.

"He'll be okay, right? He'll come back to us."

Suddenly, she felt a vibration beneath her, and in the distance, a faint muffled explosion. Atlas tensed.

"Oh, no." She couldn't just sit here. What if Boone needed help? She rose. She just needed to check was what going on. "Come on, Atlas. We'll just have a little look."

She moved back down the tunnel at a jog, praying she didn't take a wrong turn. The place was creepy as hell.

She got to the entrance and hovered at the doorway. Beside her, Atlas whined.

"I know. You're worried about him too." She stroked the dog's back. "He'll be all right."

She wanted to fall in love with Boone Hendrix. The words resonated through her. She'd already started that fall, and it was exciting, scary, exhilarating.

But it also felt right. Like coming home to where she belonged.

She shoved the metal door open, and it screeched

angrily. Then she stepped outside and tried to see down the tree-lined hillside.

Her stomach clenched. She saw smoke rising from the direction of the cabins. *No.* She heard distant shouts and squeezed her eyes closed.

Then she noted the gunfire. She sucked in a breath. That had to mean that Boone and Shep were still alive and fighting back.

Please be okay.

"Come on, Atlas." She stepped back into the gloom of the tunnel, and tugged the door closed behind her. She wouldn't put herself at risk and make things harder for Boone.

With the dog by her side, she moved back through the tunnels, taking left turns, until she reached her hiding spot.

She slid down the wall and sat with her knees up.

All she could do was wait. And pray that Boone would be safe.

He'd been in Ghost Ops. He was good at this. The best. And he had Shep helping him.

"Come back to me, Boone."

FROM THE TREES, Boone looked at the smoking ruin of one of Shep's cabins. The flames flickered greedily over the wood.

"Motherfuckers," Shep said, staring at the fire.

"Sorry, man."

"You don't need to be sorry." He hefted his rifle. "But I'll make sure those assholes regret it."

"Plan? We don't know how many are left."

"Taking down the loudmouth leader is a good place to start."

Boone nodded. "Can you see any of them?"

"No."

Boom.

Shep made a pleased sound. "Someone hit another booby-trap."

A grim smile crossed Boone's face. "Let's circle around and mark all their locations. Then we'll stop them, once and for all."

Shep nodded.

They crept quietly through the edge of the trees. Boone heard voices ahead and lifted a hand to signal Shep. His friend nodded.

He and Shep split, moving to surprise the mercenaries from two different directions.

There were three of them standing in a group. *Idiots.* It made them easy targets. One was hunched over a heavy-duty tablet.

Boone frowned. *What the hell were they doing?*

"They're closing in," one merc said.

Who was closing in? And what were they closing in on?

"In position," Shep said through the earpiece.

Boone pulled out his Glock and readied himself. "Go." He rose and fired. One merc went down with a sharp cry.

Shep rushed out of the nearby bushes like a night-

185

mare. He pounced on a second merc and dragged him down.

Boone aimed his gun at the man with the tablet. The young guy raised one hand, his other still clenched on the device.

"Good choice." Boone snatched the tablet from him, just as Shep appeared. His friend yanked the man's hands behind his back and zip-tied them.

Lifting the tablet, Boone focused on the screen. It showed an aerial view of the trees in a dark shade of blue, and there were some orange blobs in the center. Three of them in the trees and moving fast.

"What's this?" he demanded.

The young merc swallowed. "The thermal camera. It's mounted on a drone."

Boone looked up into the sky. *Shit.*

"I spotted a thermal signature up on the hillside, near the mine. Radu deduced that it was our target. That you'd hidden her."

Ice filled Boone's veins.

The merc swallowed. "He took two men, and he's moving to intercept her."

With a growl, Boone dropped the tablet and gripped the front of the man's shirt. Emotions charged through him, fear leading the way.

"Boone," Shep said sharply.

Boone met his friend's gaze.

"Go," Shep said. "I'll hold the rest off. Go get your girl."

Boone swiveled and ran.

CHAPTER SEVENTEEN

God, when would it be over? Huddled with her arms around her legs, nerves alive in her stomach, Gemma felt sick.

She shivered and wrapped her arms tighter around her body. It was cold in the tunnel.

A sound echoed off the rock walls. The screech of rusty hinges.

She shot to her feet. *Boone was back*. Her heart raced.

But beside her, Atlas growled, his strong body turning stiff. Then she heard the rumble of deep voices.

"Find her. She can't be far."

It was a familiar Romanian accent. *No*. Her stomach turned over. It wasn't Boone, it was Radu.

Shit. She glanced around. What should she do? Her fingers clenched on the gun Boone had left her.

It would be best to stay hidden. She couldn't fight off Radu and his mercenaries herself. She eyed the dark tunnel ahead of her.

"Come on, Atlas."

She set off, with Atlas right beside her. She was careful to block as much of the light from her flashlight as possible. She didn't want the mercs to spot it, but she wouldn't take the risk of trying to navigate these old tunnels in the dark either.

The tunnel inclined, going up the hill. The walls and ceiling were rough, and in places, had deteriorated. There were small piles of rubble dotted on the uneven ground.

She reached a spot where the tunnel was almost completely blocked by rock.

"Crap."

Atlas bounded up the pile of rocks, sniffed around, then wriggled his body into a narrow gap and disappeared.

Gemma carefully stepped over some large rocks and reached the hole. "Please don't collapse on me." She pulled herself in, sucking in her breath as she climbed through.

Atlas was waiting on the other side.

"Come on, boy. Let's keep moving."

Tapping down her panic rising in her throat, she kept walking through the tunnel. She just had to hide long enough for Boone to come.

She knew he'd come.

The tunnel widened, and she saw the dilapidated mine building ahead. This tunnel opened into it. Maybe she could get out of the mine and run into the trees to hide.

Voices echoed behind her in one of the side tunnels.

No. Her heart leaped into her throat. She flicked off

the flashlight. It took a few seconds for her eyes to adjust, but thankfully she saw faint light leaking in from the mine building. She gingerly moved forward.

Suddenly, Atlas made a sound.

"What is it?" she whispered.

There was a creak overhead. Without warning, rocks tumbled down on top of her.

With a cry, Gemma threw herself to the ground, covering her head with her arms. Rocks pelted her, and she breathed in dust and coughed. *Dammit.*

A sudden pain spiked through her left leg, shooting down her calf. She bit her lip to stop from crying out.

The rockfall stopped as quickly as it had started. She waved a hand to dissipate the dust. Thankfully, none of the rubble looked very large. She glanced down and gasped.

Her left leg was pinned by a small pile of rocks.

No. She tried to pull her leg free and felt a burning pain from her ankle to her knee. Trying to stay calm, she dragged in a breath. She didn't think her leg was broken, but it hurt like hell.

She started pulling the rocks off her. Atlas appeared, fur covered in dust.

"I'm okay," she whispered. She bit down hard enough that she tasted blood in her mouth. This was going to take a while.

"I heard something this way," a male voice said down the tunnel.

Shit. They were getting closer. Fear and frustration welled in her chest.

Damn. Damn. Damn.

189

She tried to yank her leg free, then heard footsteps.

She froze. She turned to Atlas' silhouette in the darkness. "Go, Atlas. Hide."

The dog hesitated, but as the men neared, he disappeared into the inky black.

Gemma pulled in a shaky breath and felt like a rock was lodged in her throat. She heard the scrape of quick moving footsteps, then a bright flashlight hit her face. She winced.

"Finally." Radu stepped forward. He was flanked by two mercenaries.

She swallowed. *Be brave. Boone will come.*

"Ms. Newhouse, you'll finally be coming with us."

She glared at him.

"Free her from the rocks," Radu ordered.

One merc moved toward her. She tightened her grip on the gun and steeled herself to actually shoot someone.

The man approached, and she whipped the gun up and fired.

He yelled, gripped his thigh, and fell.

Gemma fired more shots wildly down the tunnel.

She heard curses, then the gun was slapped out of her fingers. Radu appeared, and gripped her throat. He squeezed until she couldn't breathe.

Shit. She gasped for air.

Atlas came out of the darkness, barking and growling.

Radu lifted his gun.

"Atlas, run," she wheezed.

The merc fired, and she shoved at his legs. The shot hit the rock wall, and she caught a glimpse of the dog running into the tunnel.

Be safe, boy.

"Williams?" Radu said.

"Bullet hit my thigh."

"He's bleeding badly," the other mercenary said. "I've put my belt around it."

"Get him out of here. I'll bring the woman."

The two mercs hobbled off.

Radu crouched and started moving the rocks off her leg.

"Cause me any more trouble, and I'll beat you unconscious."

Charming. "You won't get away with this."

"I always get away, and I always get the job done. The paycheck for this job was one I couldn't turn down."

He got the last rock off her leg. Gemma whipped her legs up, ignoring a fresh surge of pain, and tried to kick him.

He knocked her legs aside, then reached over and slapped her face.

Her head rang and her eyes watered.

"Try that again." He smiled at her. "I'd really like to hit you again."

He meant it. She heard the pleasure in his voice, saw it in his face. Her chest constricted.

"Do that and I'll make you regret it."

Boone. His deep voice made her heart leap.

He came out of the darkness, gun raised.

Boom. Boom.

Gemma yelped, and watched Radu's body jerk and then collapse. He hit the rock floor hard.

She scrambled backward. "Boone!"

BOONE WATCHED IMPASSIVELY as Radu collapsed and didn't get up.

"Boone!" Gemma scrambled to her feet and almost collapsed. He caught her.

"Are you all right?" He pulled her close and breathed her in. She was alive.

"My leg was caught under some rocks, but I'm okay." She let out a shaky breath and gave him a tremulous smile. "I'm *so* happy to see you."

He pressed a hard kiss to her lips. She made a needy sound and kissed him back wildly.

When he broke the kiss, he took a second just to hold her. "Where's Atlas?"

"He ran into the tunnels. I told him to run. Radu was shooting at him."

"He'll be okay." Boone's dog was smart.

"Shep?" she asked.

"Holding off the last of the mercenaries." Boone slid a supporting arm around her. "Let's get out of here. Lean on me."

She hobbled a bit, but didn't seem to be in pain.

"*Wait.*" She gripped his vest. "There are two other mercs here. I shot one."

"*You* shot one?" God, she was something. "Don't worry about it. I took care of them already." They were trussed up in a side tunnel. He cupped her face. "Come on. Let's get you out of this damn mine."

"Yes, please."

They slowly moved down the tunnel.

When they heard a noise behind them, they both stiffened. They turned, and Boone aimed his flashlight and Glock down the tunnel.

He saw Atlas loping toward them.

Boone grinned and lowered his weapon. "Hey, you."

"*Atlas*," Gemma cried.

The dog bustled around them, and they both patted him.

"He took good care of me," she said.

Of course he did. Boone was starting to think that was the job of the Hendrix men—to protect Gemma Newhouse.

"Come on." They hobbled the rest of the way and reached the exit. He shoved the door open, and they stepped outside, blinking in the sunlight.

Boone couldn't hear any more gunfire down below, and he hoped that Shep was okay.

"It's not going to be that easy." Radu stepped out from behind a tree, gun aimed at them.

Fuck. "*Hide*," Boone barked.

Radu made a sound. "There's nowhere for you to hide."

But the command wasn't for him and Gemma. Boone knew that Atlas would have obeyed in an instant. The dog was hidden behind him and Gemma in the tunnel.

Gemma gripped Boone's side and glared at the merc.

The man had obviously used a different exit from the mine. He wasn't looking too good. He was coated in dust, with his ballistic vest hanging loose. *Damn*. Boone's bullets hadn't hurt him. Or maybe just a little. The man's left arm hung loose by his side, and Boone saw blood dripping off the man's fingers.

"Ms. Newhouse, walk to me."

She shook her head. "No. You'll shoot Boone."

"I will shoot him if you *don't* come here. Do it. *Now*."

"Go," Boone murmured.

He saw her face twist. She took two small steps toward Radu.

The merc grabbed her wrist and yanked her close. With her injured leg, he almost knocked her off balance. *Asshole.*

Radu hauled Gemma in front of him and pressed the gun against the side of her head.

Suddenly, a flashback slammed into Boone.

A Taliban soldier with his gun pressed to Julio's head as he spewed obscenities in Arabic. Boone's crushing sense of helplessness.

Breathe. You aren't in that cell. He fought to focus. *Gemma needs you. You aren't helpless this time.*

Gemma's hazel gaze came into view, locked on his. She was afraid, but she wasn't panicking. She looked at him—steady, sure, her gaze filled with trust.

She believed in him.

She knew the worst of the dark corners of his soul, and she still trusted him.

It steadied him, and his focus narrowed.

"I can't leave you alive to keep messing up my mission," Radu said.

"You need a new job," Boone suggested. "One that doesn't involve kidnapping innocent women."

"Spare me the sermon." Radu raised his gun.

"No!" Gemma cried.

Boone gave a sharp whistle, then threw himself toward the ground.

Time seemed to slow down—like everything had slid into slow motion. Gemma was yelling, and then Atlas sprinted out of the mine entrance. There was the loud report of a gun firing.

A bullet slammed into Boone's chest with the force of a sledgehammer. He grunted, knocked off his feet.

He saw Atlas slam into Radu, taking the man to the ground. The merc's screams filled the air.

Time clicked back in, and Boone landed flat on his back.

If there'd been any air left in his lungs, the fall would've knocked it out of him. But the bullet had already done that.

CHAPTER EIGHTEEN

"No, oh God. Boone." Panicked, Gemma raced across the ground and dropped down beside him. She ran her hands over him frantically.

Radu had shot him.

Boone made a low, gasping sound. "O-okay. Hit vest."

Oh. The air rushed out of her tight chest. His vest had taken the bullet. *Thank God.*

She saw him struggling to loosen the vest and helped him open it. Tears welled in her eyes.

She'd thought she'd lost him.

The world would be a much worse place without this good, honorable man in it.

Sudden gunfire made her jolt. Boone grabbed her arm.

Gemma turned her head and saw Radu, with a bloody face, firing at Atlas.

No.

But the dog was fast, zigzagging wildly. He sprinted into the trees.

Gemma's heart started to pound even harder. Radu heaved himself up, and she tried to shield Boone.

"I was told this would be an easy job. Snatch a spoiled heiress off the street, and deliver her. An easy paycheck." The merc waved his gun around, blood oozing down his cheek. "This is *not* easy." His voice rose. "When we tracked you to this man's farm, we saw he had military experience. But he was just one man, and there was nothing special in his background."

Boone rose, pulling Gemma close, and stared at the mercenary. "I was special forces."

Radu nodded. "Your background didn't mention that."

Now Boone smiled, and it raised the hairs on Gemma's arms.

"Ever heard of Ghost Ops?" Boone asked quietly.

Radu blanched.

"I guess you have. And you know what that means. It means my friend down the hill will have already dealt with your men down there." Boone's face hardened. "And I'll deal with you. There is not any option where I let you hurt her."

Radu bared his teeth. "I'm the one holding the weapon."

"I don't need a weapon."

The merc's dark eyes flared. "I think I'll tie you up, and make you watch while I hurt her."

Gemma felt Boone tense.

"I know so many interesting ways to cause pain," Radu continued.

"Try it," Boone growled.

Radu lunged forward and Boone charged to meet him, knocking Gemma out of the way. She watched him tackle Radu to the ground. The men wrestled.

The mercenary hit Boone in the chest, and she gasped. The asshole was trying to hit Boone where he was hurt. She saw Boone flinch, but he didn't loosen his hold on the man. He reared his head back and head-butted Radu. The mercenary made an angry sound.

Gemma looked around for a weapon. There was nothing, dammit. Then she spied a good-sized rock. She snatched it up and hurried over to where the men rolled in the dirt. She slammed the rock down into Radu's back.

The mercenary cursed. She hit him again.

The men rolled a few more times, the fight vicious. It was all elbows, grappling, and grunts. Radu broke free and rose, blood smeared on his teeth, and his dark hair mussed.

Boone leaped up.

Then Radu held up an object, and she saw Boone freeze.

Oh, hell. It was a grenade.

Radu smiled. "It seems I do have an option where I get to hurt her."

God. What did they do now? Her heart hammered against her ribs, and she met Boone's gaze.

"Boone, I need to tell you something." She swallowed. She had to tell him. She might not get another chance. "I'm falling in love with you."

His head jerked. "Gemma—"

"Shut up," Radu said. "In a few seconds, you'll be

dead, and I'll be dragging her by the hair to my employer."

"That won't be happening today," a cool, lethal voice said.

Gemma's head whipped up. A man stepped out of the trees dressed in black tactical gear, a rifle up and aimed at Radu. His face was handsome, but that wasn't the first thing she noticed. The first thing was the dangerous intensity emanating off him.

She gasped. Vander Norcross.

Shep stepped out on Vander's left. Another man appeared on his right—Declan Ward.

Several other people, all carrying rifles, emerged from the trees. She recognized Cal Ward, who was accompanied by a big man with hair almost to his shoulders, and a tall, dangerous-looking woman with black hair. Gemma guessed they were all members of Treasure Hunter Security.

Radu's face twisted and his arm moved to pull the pin on the grenade.

"Don't," Vander clipped.

Shep fired. The bullet caught Radu in his right arm. He dropped the grenade, and it fell harmlessly to the ground.

Boone reached for Gemma, and she wrapped her arms around him.

"Once again, your timing is spot on, Shep," Boone said dryly.

Shep shrugged. "Someone has to save your ass."

Boone smiled. "Glad you did."

SITTING ON THE GRASS, Boone pulled his vest off. Fuck, his chest hurt.

Gemma crouched beside him, worry etched on her face. "Boone."

He ignored the others as they secured Radu and pulled her onto his lap. Then he tipped her head back and kissed her.

She made a sound, her hand curling around his neck. She kissed him back until he heard a sob escape her.

"Baby." He pressed his nose to hers. "It's all okay, now."

"I thought he'd killed you." Her gaze met his, glimmering with tears. "I can't lose you."

His chest was so damn tight. He tugged her closer. "Why?"

"You know why." She pressed her forehead to his.

"Tell me again."

"Because I'm falling in love with you."

Damn. He felt like his chest expanded several times over. It felt so good to hear that, and to see it shining in her pretty eyes.

For a long time, he hadn't wanted to feel. Hell, he couldn't feel because he'd been numb and drowning in guilt.

Now Gemma had opened up something inside him.

"I'm falling in love with you, too," he told her.

With a cry, she pressed her lips to his.

He kissed her hungrily. She was safe. *Finally.* And she loved him.

It was the best feeling in the world.

He pulled back and saw Vander watching them. His old commander raised a brow.

"Any injuries, you two?" Declan asked.

Gemma nodded. "Boone was shot."

"Just a bullet to the vest. I'm fine." He accepted Declan's hand to get up. "Gemma's leg got caught under some rocks. It got banged up."

"Just scratches. It'll keep for now." She leaned into him.

"Shep?" Boone said. "You all right?"

His friend strode over. "All good."

Boone slapped his friend's shoulder, incredibly grateful for his help. Then Boone looked at Declan. "Thanks for coming."

The man nodded. "I grabbed my team, and we flew up in a helo."

"I owe you." Then he turned to Vander. "I didn't expect to see you here."

"After you were attacked in Denver, I decided to pop in for a visit." He glanced around, his gaze hitting Radu and turning Arctic. "Glad I did."

Boone slid an arm around Gemma. "She safe now?"

Vander nodded. "It's over."

Gemma straightened. "Really?"

"William Carruthers was arrested by the British police today."

Gemma jolted, and Boone squeezed the back of her neck. "That's good news."

"It's really over," she whispered.

Vander nodded. "Your father pulled a lot of strings

and called in a lot of favors. Once it was uncovered that Carruthers was behind your abduction, your father wouldn't rest until he was taken down."

Her lips parted. "Dad did that?"

"He did. And he's here. He demanded to come and see that you were safe."

"Dad's here?" She glanced down the hill.

"He's waiting down at the cabins," Vander added.

Suddenly, there was rustling in the nearby bushes. Everyone swiveled and snapped their weapons up.

A German Shepherd bounded out of the trees, and made a beeline for Boone and Gemma.

Boone smiled, relief hitting him.

"Atlas!" Gemma beamed at the dog.

They both patted him, and his tail wagged madly. Gemma crouched and hugged the dog's neck.

"This guy right here was one of my heroes today."

Boone rubbed Atlas between the ears. "Good work, boy."

"He's earned a year's worth of dog treats," Gemma said.

"What about me?" Boone complained.

She shot him a sexy smile. "Oh, you'll get a special thank you. Don't worry."

He felt a throb of desire that he fought for control. "You really falling in love with me?"

Her lips pressed together, and she nodded.

"How do you feel about living in Vermont?" He knew that both he and Atlas could never make a home in LA, but he'd do whatever he needed to do to make Gemma happy.

"I like it a lot," she said. "As long as I have you, I don't care where we are." She smiled. "Oh, and I need a kitchen so I can bake."

"It just so happens that I have the kitchen."

"I know."

"And I'm really ready to fall the rest of the way in love with you."

He saw warmth fill her eyes. He kissed her again, pulling in the sweet taste of her.

"Sorry to interrupt." Vander's voice was faintly amused. "I think you'd better head down and let your father know that you're all right."

Gemma nodded and took Boone's hand.

Right, time to meet a billionaire. One whose daughter he was sleeping with.

Boone suddenly felt more uneasy than when he'd faced down the mercenaries. But nothing and no one would keep him from Gemma.

AS THEY STEPPED into Shep's clearing, Gemma glanced around.

Oh, God. Her fingers clenched on Boone's hand. The cabin closest to them was riddled with bullet holes. Another one was a wreck and still on fire.

"Shep, I'm so sorry. I'll cover the cost of all of this."

Boone's friend shook his head. "It's nothing I can't fix."

She saw several mercenaries sitting on the ground with their hands and feet zip-tied. A handsome black man, and a lean man with pitch-black hair were watching them. More of Declan's team. There were also several bodies laid out under white sheets.

She averted her gaze. She was damn glad that Carruthers would pay for all of this.

Then she saw the sleek, gray SUV parked in front of Shep's cabin—a Lamborghini Urus. Her father stood beside it with two of his security team. Her dad looked worried.

When he spotted her, his face changed. "*Gemma.*"

"Go," Boone urged her.

She ran to her dad, and was engulfed in his arms.

"Jesus, we were so worried." He hugged her hard.

"I'm all right, Dad. I promise."

He pulled back, his gaze searching her face. "You're sure?"

She smiled. "I'm sure. It got pretty..." Her voice cracked.

He hugged her again. "We need to call your mom. Let her know that you're safe. She's been worried sick. She wanted to come, but I made her stay in LA."

Tears welled in Gemma's eyes. For all their faults, and hers, her parents loved her. They were family. She had to stop expecting them to match some fantasy version of parents, and just accept them as they were.

"I wouldn't have made it alone, Dad."

"I know." His gaze lifted and moved over her shoulder.

She turned and saw Boone standing there.

"Dad, this is Boone Hendrix. Boone, my father, Paul Newhouse."

"Thank you, Boone." Her dad held out a hand and the men shook. "I owe you more than I can ever tell you."

"It's a pleasure to meet you, Mr. Newhouse," Boone said.

"Call me Paul. I'll be giving you a sizable reward."

She saw Boone stiffen. "I don't want a reward."

"You've earned it."

"No." Boone's tone was sharp.

Gemma hid her smile. She reached out her hand and Boone took it, their fingers tangling.

Her father's gaze dropped to their linked hands, and his brow creased. Then he got a blank look that she knew well—his business face.

"Ah." Her father nodded. "I see you want an even bigger reward."

"Yes, I do," Boone said.

Gemma frowned. "Dad—"

"Fine." Her father held up a hand, his gaze locked on Boone. "I'll cut you a check. One million dollars."

Gemma gasped. For one horrible second, she was a teenager again, discovering that the boy she cared about was only interested in her because of her dad's money.

"Take the money, Hendrix, and leave my daughter alone."

Boone shook his head. "When I said a bigger reward, I didn't mean money, Newhouse. I meant Gemma."

She jolted.

Boone turned to her. "Gemma, I've been closed off from life for a long time. I didn't want to feel or care. I didn't want to risk losing another person I loved."

Her insides melted.

"But from the moment I pulled you from my river, you've given me no choice." He cupped her cheeks. "You charmed me, made me smile, baked me delicious things."

She laughed.

"Most of all, you made me feel. You made me want. You dragged me back to life. Every day, you amaze me with your strength and kindness. I could be offered a hundred million dollars, hell, a billion dollars, and you're still worth more to me. I'm not sure I'm good enough for you—"

She gripped his wrists. "You are. You absolutely are."

"All I can promise is to love you. To keep you safe. And every day, work my damned hardest to make you happy."

"Oh, Boone."

"Hell of a speech."

Gemma didn't look away from Boone, but she recognized Shep's voice.

"Sure was," Vander agreed.

She ignored them, and dragged Boone's head down for a kiss. She didn't hold back, pouring everything she felt into it.

When they finally broke apart, she licked her lips, and they shared a smile.

Then anger hit her. She turned to face her father...

Only to find him smiling at them.

He held out a hand to Boone. "Welcome to the family."

Gemma frowned. "That was a test?"

"You've been hurt before by men who weren't worthy of you. Not letting it happen again."

She sighed. "Dad..."

He touched her cheek. "I love you, Gem. And I think you've finally found a man who'll love you like you deserve."

SHEP WATCHED as the FBI agents rounded up the mercenaries. Gemma's father had worked some sort of magic with law enforcement, claiming Boone and Shep were part of her security team.

Hell of a day. He eyed the still-smoldering ruin of the cabin. This definitely wasn't what he'd expected when he'd woken up today.

He realized how much he'd missed the work. He'd been a damn good soldier, and it had suited him. Today, working side-by-side with Boone again had felt good.

He glanced over at his friend. Boone had his woman wrapped up tightly in his arms. He looked happy. He'd earned some good. Shep knew better than anyone that Boone had watched their friends die, been through hell, and come out the other side.

Yeah, Boone Hendrix had finally found a woman who deserved him.

Not that Shep wanted a woman. *Fuck, no.*

He liked being alone.

He had a few people he trusted, and that was enough for him. He could see Boone was happy, and Gemma was one-of-a-kind, but it didn't mean he wanted that for himself.

Boone had left the military with survivor's guilt, and

Shep had come back with a reminder that he'd been too fucking late.

Again.

It was a repeating theme in his life.

Up here in the mountains, there was no one depending on him.

"You did good work today, Shep." Vander appeared out of nowhere.

Shep had always hated when the man did that. "I'll always help my brothers."

"I know." His old commander paused, scanning the clearing. "You know, I always have work for you if you're interested."

Norcross Security was based in San Francisco, but Shep knew they did work all across the country.

He watched the mercs being loaded into big black Suburbans. He had liked using his skills today, but the thought of being back on a team, protecting others, having their backs 24/7...

"I'm good. I like the retired life."

Vander's dark gaze bored into him, and Shep fought the urge to hunch his shoulders. Vander had that kind of laser look that made it feel like he could see right into your brain.

"We couldn't have saved Julio, Miles, and Charlie, Shep," Vander said quietly.

Shep's jaw tightened. He stayed silent.

"Do you blame Boone for not saving them?"

"No," Shep clipped. "He was locked in a fucking cage. I wasn't."

"Do you blame me?"

"Hell, no. I saw you turn yourself inside out to find them."

"You did, too. So how the fuck can you blame yourself?"

How he felt wasn't exactly rational. Shep knew that. It was a dark, ugly feeling that lived inside him, feeding off old hurts.

"Can we drop it?" Shep dealt with it best by not thinking about it.

The fact was, Julio, Miles, and Charlie weren't the only people Shep had been too late to save.

"I won't let you hide up here, stewing on shit that wasn't your fault," Vander said with an edge to his voice. "That's a promise."

Vander shot him a hard look, then swiveled and headed over to talk to the FBI.

Shep released a breath. *Fuck.* When Vander Norcross made a promise, he kept it.

Fucking fuck.

No. Nothing was going to get him to leave his mountain. He was where he needed to be. Alone, with no dramas, no hassles, and no responsibilities.

CHAPTER NINETEEN

B oone swung the axe, chopping the log cleanly. He needed more wood for the fire.

Snow had been falling for the last few days, leaving the farm coated in white. Although today, they had a blue sky and some sunshine.

He smiled. Lately, chopping wood wasn't always about escaping from his demons. Sure, he still had some nightmares and bad moments which sent him out here to punish the logs. But mostly, he just came out here to chop wood to keep the fire burning and Gemma smiling.

His smile widened. His new favorite pastime was making love to her in front of the fireplace. She always locked poor Atlas in the bedroom first.

Christmas was coming soon. For the first time in years, he was excited for the holiday. He'd already cut down a tree with Gemma. She'd taken over an hour to pick the perfect one. She had plans to cook and bake and decorate.

The last few weeks together had been some of the happiest of his life.

The best thing was that Gemma seemed to love it here. She baked a lot, testing and formulating new recipes. She was planning to open her bakery sometime in the new year, although she still hadn't committed to a date. He could tell she was still a little nervous, although her father had helped her with the business plan.

As she'd predicted, Paul tried to be over ambitious and started talking about expansion opportunities. After a few heated discussions, she'd managed to convince him that she wanted to keep her bakery small and intimate.

She had started a Vermont chapter of Angel Cakes. Every week she baked a cake or two to take to local hospitals, sick kids, and foster homes. She made him so damn proud that she was his.

Yes, he was happy. He looked up at the winter sun. He knew that Julio, Charlie, and Miles were smiling down at him.

Gemma's parents were coming for a visit in the new year. Boone winced. He was sure it would be fine, but he wasn't convinced that rural Vermont was the Newhouses' scene.

Luckily, her father had some business events to attend, so they'd only be staying a few days.

Toward the end of January, Boone was taking Gemma to meet Julio's family. She'd already promised to bake Eddie a chocolate cake. Oh, and she'd almost convinced a grumpy Shep to come and visit them in Vermont, too.

Today, Boone had a gift to give to Gemma. Christmas

was still too far away, and he didn't want to wait any longer to give it to her.

He heard the cabin door open, then Atlas' happy woof.

He set the axe down and turned. Atlas pranced through the snow, and Gemma followed behind the dog, wrapped in a loose cardigan and leggings, her feet in a pair of Boone's boots. She had a red knit hat covering her hair and was carrying two mugs of hot chocolate. Best of all, she was smiling at him.

His chest swelled, and he knew exactly what that feeling was—happiness. Pure happiness threaded with love.

"Good morning, Ms. Newhouse."

"Morning."

He took the mugs from her and set them on one of the logs. When he straightened, she leaped into his arms and wrapped her legs around his waist.

He took her mouth in a deep, lazy kiss. She tasted like hot chocolate and peppermint, which she called her Christmas Candy Cane hot chocolate. He cupped her lovely ass as she speared her fingers into his hair.

She nibbled on his lips. "I like the way you say good morning."

He watched the way the sunlight lit up her pretty face. "Thank you."

She blinked. "For what?"

"For bringing me back to life. For loving me."

Her face softened. "You don't need to thank me, Boone. You make it easy."

He kissed her again, his mouth traveling down the

side of her neck. "I think we should head back to bed for a bit and warm up. It's pretty cold this morning."

She made a humming noise. "I like your thinking. Safety first and all."

A thunking noise made them look down. Atlas had knocked over the hot chocolate mugs and was lapping at the spill.

Gemma laughed. "That dog is way too smart."

"Atlas, no," Boone said. "That's no good for you."

The dog sat back and gave them a sad look.

Gemma pulled something from her pocket. It was a baked dog treat. "A carob treat just for you." She tossed it.

Atlas nabbed it fast.

"That'll keep him busy for a bit." Boone hitched her higher and carried her toward the cabin.

GEMMA PULLED the tray of freshly baked cupcakes out of the oven. Mmm, they smelled good. Next, she pulled out a tray of dog treats too. These were a new flavor for Atlas to try—peanut butter and pumpkin with bacon glaze. They were shaped like little dog paws.

After Boone had carried her back to bed for an hour this morning—a very pleasurable hour for both of them—he'd headed out to the barn. Declan had organized for Boone's uncle's truck to be shipped back from Denver. Boone was repairing the bullet holes in it himself.

She loved popping out there to watch him. She could picture him now, leaning under the open hood, denim cupping his magnificent ass.

She laughed. Fantasizing about Boone, and then making those fantasies a reality, was one of her new favorite pastimes. She touched the stubble burn on her neck. She had it in a few other places too.

She was so in love.

So happy she could burst.

Her gaze dropped to the cooling cupcakes and her belly clenched. Okay, there was one little niggle.

She had a business plan for the bakery done, and she had a bunch of recipes prepared and ready to go.

But she was still dragging her feet.

Butterflies took flight in her belly. It was easy just to stay busy, settling into her new home in Vermont, and enjoying her time with Boone.

Deep down, she was still afraid of taking a risk and failing. Not financially. She was fortunate that wasn't something she had to worry about. No, she was afraid of putting her passion—something she loved—out there, and people not loving it back.

She heard the back door to the mudroom open, then Boone stomping snow off his boots. He appeared, the red flannel shirt she loved hugging his chest.

"Smells good in here." He saw the cupcakes and his face lit up.

"They're not ready yet," she told him. "I need to make the frosting."

A wicked smile crossed his rugged face. "I could help."

A full-body shiver moved through her. She kept waiting for this heat between them to mellow, but it just seemed to get stronger. "I might let you."

"Actually, I need you to grab your coat and boots. I have something to show you."

She raised a brow.

"A gift." He held up some black fabric. "But I need to blindfold you first."

She laughed. "What?"

"It's a surprise." Stepping up behind her, he put the fabric over her eyes and tied it behind her head. "Trust me?"

Her heart swelled. "Always."

After they'd put their winter gear on, he led her carefully out to the truck, and whistled for Atlas.

"Boone, where are we going?"

He helped her into the seat and fastened the seatbelt. "Not far."

It was a short drive and when he finally stopped the truck, she was feeling a tiny bit nervous. "This is a little bit kinky, Boone."

He opened the passenger door. "No peeking," he warned.

Gemma held onto his hand as he helped her from the truck. She clung to him as they walked across what felt like gravel. Nearby, Atlas made an excited noise. *Where were they?*

"Okay, you can look now." He loosened the blindfold.

She blinked at the light. The temperature had dropped from the sunny morning, so she was bundled up in her favorite coat, scarf, and hat. She saw May and Frank's general store. The couple were at the window, waving at them.

ANNA HACKETT

She smiled and waved back. She'd gotten to know the pair quite well since she'd moved to Vermont.

Boone turned her to face the stone building beside the store. It looked like it had once been a shop or café of some kind, but was now empty.

"What is this place?" she asked.

"It's yours. For your bakery."

Her mouth dropped open. She was speechless. He'd known. Known she was nervous and dragging her feet. Known that she just needed a little push...with him at her side.

"Boone..."

"There's decent traffic on this road, and a lot of locals come to the general store. You'll get a good number of customers."

She nodded.

"Come on." He grabbed her hand and led her to the door. He pulled out some keys and unlocked it.

There was a musty smell inside, but she instantly saw the charm and possibilities. The large windows at the front would let in great light, and the place had lovely wooden floors, even if they did need to be refinished.

"It needs some paint and attention, but this would be a good storefront." He towed her around the counter and through a door. "There's a large kitchen back here. We'll need to put in your ovens. And whatever else you want."

Her heart swelled as she turned in a slow circle. The place was dusty, and there were cobwebs in the corners, but in her head, she saw her shining bakery.

Boone believed in her. No questions. No hesitation. He had her back, and he loved her.

She knew he'd love her even if she failed, or if she was wildly successful. If it didn't work out, he'd catch her and help her get back up. If it went well, he'd celebrate her success.

"I love it." Tears welled.

He took her face in his hands and brushed the tears away with his thumbs. "Gemma's Bakery. It'll have the best cupcakes in Vermont."

"And it will also specialize in baked dog treats. Atlas will be the official taste tester." She smiled. "I want a little area where people can bring their dogs."

"That's a brilliant idea."

She pressed her hands to his chest. "I love the place, Boone, but not half as much as I love you."

He lowered his head and got busy kissing her.

The door jingled and Atlas appeared. Gemma still couldn't believe the dog could open doors. Atlas leaned his weight against them, almost knocking them off balance.

"Atlas," Boone growled.

"He just wants some love and attention." She rubbed the dog's flank. "Don't you, boy?"

Atlas licked her hand and she laughed.

"Atlas needs a woman of his own, so he stops hogging mine." Boone swung her into his arms.

Gemma gasped and slid an arm across his broad shoulders. "Don't worry, Boone, you're the love of my life."

"And you're the love of mine, Gemma. My love, my heart, my light."

She smiled, loving when her protective hero was

sweet. She pressed her lips to his temple. She knew whatever life held for them, it would be bright.

I hope you enjoyed Boone and Gemma's story!

Unbroken Heroes continues with *The Hero She Wants*, starring grumpy loner Shep Barlow. Coming January 2024.

If you'd like to know more about **Declan Ward** and the Treasure Hunter Security team**,** then check out the Treasure Hunter Security series, starting with *Undiscovered* (Declan and Layne's story).

If you'd like to know more about **Vander Norcross,** then check out the first Norcross Security book, *The Investigator*. **Read on for a preview of the first chapter.**

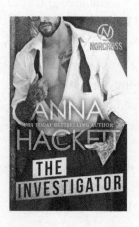

THE HERO SHE NEEDS

Don't miss out! For updates about new releases, free books, and other fun stuff, sign up for my VIP mailing list and get your *free box set* containing three action-packed romances.

Visit here to get started: www.annahackett.com

Would you like
a FREE BOX SET
of my books?

PREVIEW: THE INVESTIGATOR

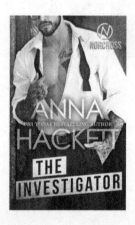

There was a glass of chardonnay with her name on it waiting for her at home.

Haven McKinney smiled. The museum was closed, and she was *done* for the day.

As she walked across the East gallery of the Hutton Museum, her heels clicked on the marble floor.

God, she loved the place. The creamy marble that made up the flooring and wrapped around the grand pillars was gorgeous. It had that hushed air of grandeur that made her heart squeeze a little every time she stepped inside. But more than that, the amazing art the Hutton housed sang to the art lover in her blood.

Snagging a job here as the curator six months ago had been a dream come true. She'd been at a low point in her life. Very low. Haven swallowed a snort and circled a stunning white-marble sculpture of a naked, reclining woman with the most perfect resting bitch face. She'd never guessed that her life would come crashing down at age twenty-nine.

She lifted her chin. Miami was her past. The Hutton and San Francisco were her future. No more throwing caution to the wind. She had a plan, and she was sticking to it.

She paused in front of a stunning exhibit of traditional Chinese painting and calligraphy. It was one of their newer exhibits, and had been Haven's brainchild. Nearby, an interactive display was partially assembled. Over the next few days, her staff would finish the installation. Excitement zipped through Haven. She couldn't wait to have the touchscreens operational. It was her passion to make art more accessible, especially to children. To help them be a part of it, not just look at it. To learn, to feel, to enjoy.

Art had helped her through some of the toughest times in her life, and she wanted to share that with others.

She looked at the gorgeous old paintings again. One portrayed a mountainous landscape with beautiful maple trees. It soothed her nerves.

Wine would soothe her nerves, as well. *Right*. She

needed to get upstairs to her office and grab her handbag, then get an Uber home.

Her cell phone rang and she unclipped it from the lanyard she wore at the museum. "Hello?"

"Change of plans, girlfriend," a smoky female voice said. "Let's go out and celebrate being gorgeous, successful, and single. I'm done at the office, and believe me, it has been a *grueling* day."

Haven smiled at her new best friend. She'd met Gia Norcross when she joined the Hutton. Gia's wealthy brother, Easton Norcross, owned the museum, and was Haven's boss. The museum was just a small asset in the businessman's empire. Haven suspected Easton owned at least a third of San Francisco. Maybe half.

She liked and respected her boss. Easton could be tough, but he valued her opinions. And she loved his bossy, take-charge, energetic sister. Gia ran a highly successful PR firm in the city, and did all the PR and advertising for the Hutton. They'd met not long after Haven had started work at the museum.

After their first meeting, Gia had dragged Haven out to her favorite restaurant and bar, and the rest was history.

"I guess making people's Instagram look pretty and not staged is hard work," Haven said with a grin.

"Bitch." Gia laughed. "God, I had a meeting with a businessman caught in...well, let's just say he and his assistant were *not* taking notes on the boardroom table."

Haven felt an old, unwelcome memory rise up. She mentally stomped it down. "I don't feel sorry for the cheating asshole, I feel sorry for whatever poor shmuck got more than they were paid for when they walked into the boardroom."

"Actually, it was the cheating businessman's wife."

"Uh-oh."

"And the assistant was male," Gia added.

"Double uh-oh."

"Then said cheater comes to my PR firm, telling me to clean up his mess, because he's thinking he might run for governor one day. I mean, I'm good, but I can't wrangle miracles."

Haven suspected that Gia had verbally eviscerated the man and sent him on his way. Gia Norcross had a sharp tongue, and wasn't afraid to use it.

"So, grueling day and I need alcohol. I'll meet you at ONE65, and the first drink is on me."

"I'm pretty wiped, Gia—"

"Uh-uh, no excuses. I'll see you in an hour." And with that, Gia was gone.

Haven clipped her phone to her lanyard. Well, it looked like she was having that chardonnay at ONE65, the six-story, French dining experience Gia loved. Each level offered something different, from patisserie, to bistro and grill, to bar and lounge.

Haven walked into the museum's main gallery, and her blood pressure dropped to a more normal level. It was her favorite space in the museum. The smell of wood, the gorgeous lights gleaming overhead, and the amazing paintings combined to create a soothing room. She smoothed her hands down her fitted, black skirt. Haven was tall, at five foot eight, and curvy, just like her mom had been. Her boobs, currently covered by a cute, white blouse with a tie around her neck, weren't much to write home about, but she had to buy her skirts one size bigger. She sighed. No matter how much she walked or jogged —*blergh*, okay, she didn't jog much—she still had an ass.

Even in her last couple of months in Miami, when stress had caused her to lose a bunch of weight due to everything going on, her ass hadn't budged.

Memories of Miami—and her douchebag-of-epic-proportions-ex—threatened, churning like storm clouds on the horizon.

Nope. She locked those thoughts down. She was *not* going there.

She had a plan, and the number one thing for taking back and rebuilding her life was *no* men. She'd sworn off anyone with a Y chromosome.

She didn't need one, didn't want one, she was D-O-N-E, done.

She stopped in front of the museum's star attraction. Claude Monet's *Water Lilies*.

Haven loved the impressionist's work. She loved the colors, the delicate strokes. This one depicted water lilies and lily pads floating on a gentle pond. His paintings always made an impact, and had a haunting, yet soothing feel to them.

It was also worth just over a hundred million dollars.

The price tag still made her heart flutter. She'd put a business case to Easton, and they'd purchased the painting three weeks ago at auction. Haven had planned out the display down to the rivets used on the wood. She'd thrown herself into the project.

Gia had put together a killer marketing campaign,

and Haven had reluctantly been interviewed by the local paper. But it had paid off. Ticket sales to the museum were up, and everyone wanted to see *Water Lilies*.

Footsteps echoed through the empty museum, and she turned to see a uniformed security guard appear in the doorway.

"Ms. McKinney?"

"Yes, David? I was just getting ready to leave."

"Sorry to delay you. There's a delivery truck at the back entrance. They say they have a delivery of a Zadkine bronze."

Haven frowned, running through the next day's schedule in her head. "That's due tomorrow."

"It sounds like they had some other deliveries nearby and thought they'd squeeze it in."

She glanced at her slim, silver wristwatch, fighting back annoyance. She'd had a long day, and now she'd be late to meet Gia. "Fine. Have them bring it in."

With a nod, David disappeared. Haven pulled out her phone and quickly fired off a text to warn Gia that she'd be late. Then Haven headed up to her office, and checked her notes for tomorrow. She had several calls to make to chase down some pieces for a new exhibit she wanted to launch in the winter. There were some restoration quotes to go over, and a charity gala for her art charity to plan. She needed to get down into the storage rooms and see if there was anything they could cycle out and put on display.

God, she loved her job. Not many people would get excited about digging around in dusty storage rooms, but Haven couldn't wait.

She made sure her laptop was off and grabbed her handbag. She slipped her lanyard off and stuffed her phone in her bag.

When she reached the bottom of the stairs, she heard a strange noise from the gallery. A muffled pop, then a thump.

Frowning, she took one step toward the gallery.

Suddenly, David staggered through the doorway, a splotch of red on his shirt.

Haven's pulse spiked. *Oh God, was that blood?* "David—"

"Run." He collapsed to the floor.

Fear choking her, she kicked off her heels and spun. She had to get help.

But she'd only taken two steps when a hand sank into her hair, pulling her neat twist loose, and sending her brown hair cascading over her shoulders.

"Let me go!"

She was dragged into the main gallery, and when she lifted her head, her gut churned.

Five men dressed in black, all wearing balaclavas, stood in a small group.

No...oh, no.

Their other guard, Gus, stood with his hands in the air. He was older, former military. She was shoved closer toward him.

"Ms. McKinney, you okay?" Gus asked.

She managed a nod. "They shot David."

"I kn—"

"No talking," one man growled.

Haven lifted her chin. "What do you want?" There was a slight quaver in her voice.

The man who'd grabbed her glared. His cold, blue eyes glittered through the slits in his balaclava. Then he ignored her, and with the others, they turned to face the *Water Lilies*.

Haven's stomach dropped. *No.* This couldn't be happening.

A thin man moved forward, studying the painting's gilt frame with gloved hands. "It's wired to an alarm."

Blue Eyes, clearly the group's leader, turned and aimed the gun at Gus' barrel chest. "Disconnect it."

"No," the guard said belligerently.

"I'm not asking."

Haven held up her hands. "Please—"

The gun fired. Gus dropped to one knee, pressing a hand to his shoulder.

"No!" she cried.

The leader stepped forward and pressed the gun to the older man's head.

"No." Haven fought back her fear and panic. "Don't hurt him. I'll disconnect it."

Slowly, she inched toward the painting, carefully avoiding the thin man still standing close to it. She touched the security panel built in beside the frame, pressing her palm to the small pad.

A second later, there was a discreet beep.

Two other men came forward and grabbed the frame.

She glanced around at them. "You're making a mistake. If you know who owns this museum, then you know you won't get away with this." Who would go up against the Norcross family? Easton, rich as sin, had a lot of connections, but his brother, Vander... Haven suppressed a shiver. Gia's middle brother might be hot, but he scared the bejesus out of Haven.

Vander Norcross, former military badass, owned Norcross Security and Investigations. His team had put in the high-tech security for the museum.

No one in their right mind wanted to go up against Vander, or the third Norcross brother who also worked with Vander, or the rest of Vander's team of badasses.

"Look, if you just—"

The blow to her head made her stagger. She blinked, pain radiating through her face. Blue Eyes had back-handed her.

He moved in and hit her again, and Haven cried out, clutching her face. It wasn't the first time she'd been hit. Her douchebag ex had hit her once. That was the day she'd left him for good.

But this was worse. Way worse.

"Shut up, you stupid bitch."

The next blow sent her to the floor. She thought she heard someone chuckle. He followed with a kick to her ribs, and Haven curled into a ball, a sob in her throat.

Her vision wavered and she blinked. Blue Eyes crouched down, putting his hand to the tiles right in front of her. Dizziness hit her, and she vaguely took in the freckles on the man's hand. They formed a spiral pattern.

"No one talks back to me," the man growled. "Especially a woman." He moved away.

She saw the men were busy maneuvering the painting off the wall. It was easy for two people to move.

She knew its exact dimensions—eighty by one hundred centimeters.

No one was paying any attention to her. Fighting through the nausea and dizziness, she dragged herself a few inches across the floor, closer to the nearby pillar. A pillar that had one of several hidden, high-tech panic buttons built into it.

When the men were turned away, she reached up and pressed the button.

Then blackness sucked her under.

———

HAVEN SAT on one of the lovely wooden benches she'd had installed around the museum. She'd wanted somewhere for guests to sit and take in the art.

She'd never expected to be sitting on one, holding a melting ice pack to her throbbing face, and staring at the empty wall where a multi-million-dollar masterpiece should be hanging. And she definitely didn't expect to be doing it with police dusting black powder all over the museum's walls.

Tears pricked her eyes. She was alive, her guards were hurt but alive, and that was what mattered. The police had questioned her and she'd told them everything she could remember. The paramedics had checked her over and given her the ice pack. Nothing was broken, but she'd been told to expect swelling and bruising.

David and Gus had been taken to the hospital. She'd been assured the men would be okay. Last she'd heard, David was in surgery. Her throat tightened. *Oh, God.*

What was she going to tell Easton?

Haven bit her lip and a tear fell down her cheek. She hadn't cried in months. She'd shed more than enough tears over Leo after he'd gone crazy and hit her. She'd left Miami the next day. She'd needed to get away from her ex and, unfortunately, despite loving her job at a classy Miami art gallery, Leo's cousin had owned it. Alyssa had been the one who had introduced them.

Haven had learned a painful lesson to not mix business and pleasure.

She'd been done with Leo's growing moodiness, outbursts, and cheating on her and hitting her had been the last straw. *Asshole.*

She wiped the tear away. San Francisco was as far from Miami as she could get and still be in the continental US. This was supposed to be her fresh new start.

She heard footsteps—solid, quick, and purposeful. Easton strode in.

He was a tall man, with dark hair that curled at the collar of his perfectly fitted suit. Haven had sworn off men, but she was still woman enough to appreciate her boss' good looks. His mother was Italian-American, and she'd passed down her very good genes to her children.

Like his brothers, Easton had been in the military, too, although he'd joined the Army Rangers. It showed in his muscled body. Once, she'd seen his shirt sleeves rolled up when they'd had a late meeting. He had some interesting ink that was totally at odds with his sophisticated-businessman persona.

His gaze swept the room, his jaw tight. It settled on her and he strode over.

"Haven—"

"Oh God, Easton. I'm so sorry."

He sat beside her and took her free hand. He squeezed her cold fingers, then he looked at her face and cursed.

She hadn't been brave enough to look in the mirror, but she guessed it was bad.

"They took the *Water Lilies*," she said.

"Okay, don't worry about it just now."

She gave a hiccupping laugh. "Don't worry? It's worth a hundred and ten *million* dollars."

A muscle ticked in his jaw. "You're okay, and that's the main thing. And the guards are in serious but stable condition at the hospital."

She nodded numbly. "It's all my fault."

Easton's gaze went to the police, and then moved back to her. "That's not true."

"I let them in." Her voice broke. God, she wanted the marble floor to crack and swallow her.

"Don't worry." Easton's face turned very serious. "Vander and Rhys will find the painting."

Her boss' tone made her shiver. Something made her suspect that Easton wanted his brothers to find the men who'd stolen the painting more than recovering the priceless piece of art.

She licked her lips, and felt the skin on her cheek tug. She'd have some spectacular bruises later. *Great. Thanks, universe.*

Then Easton's head jerked up, and Haven followed his gaze.

A man stood in the doorway. She hadn't heard him

coming. Nope, Vander Norcross moved silently, like a ghost.

He was a few inches over six feet, had a powerful body, and radiated authority. His suit didn't do much to tone down the sense that a predator had stalked into the room. While Easton was handsome, Vander wasn't. His face was too rugged, and while both he and Easton had blue eyes, Vander's were dark indigo, and as cold as the deepest ocean depths.

He didn't look happy. She fought back a shiver.

Then another man stepped up beside Vander.

Haven's chest locked. *Oh, no. No, no, no.*

She should have known. He was Vander's top investigator. Rhys Matteo Norcross, the youngest of the Norcross brothers.

At first glance, he looked like his brothers—similar build, muscular body, dark hair and bronze skin. But Rhys was the youngest, and he had a charming edge his brothers didn't share. He smiled more frequently, and his shaggy, thick hair always made her imagine him as a rock star, holding a guitar and making girls scream.

Haven was also totally, one hundred percent in lust with him. Any time he got near, he made her body flare to life, her heart beat faster, and made her brain freeze up. She could barely talk around the man.

She did *not* want Rhys Norcross to notice her. Or talk to her. Or turn his soulful, brown eyes her way.

Nuh-uh. No way. She'd sworn off men. This one should have a giant warning sign hanging on him. *Watch out, heartbreak waiting to happen.*

Rhys had been in the military with Vander. Some

hush-hush special unit that no one talked about. Now he worked at Norcross Security—apparently finding anything and anyone.

He also raced cars and boats in his free time. The man liked to go fast. Oh, and he bedded women. His reputation was legendary. Rhys liked a variety of adventures and experiences.

It was lucky Haven had sworn off men.

Especially when they happened to be her boss' brother.

And especially, especially when they were also her best friend's brother.

Off limits.

She saw the pair turn to look her and Easton's way.

Crap. Pulse racing, she looked at her bare feet and red toenails, which made her realize she hadn't recovered her shoes yet. They were her favorites.

She felt the men looking at her, and like she was drawn by a magnet, she looked up. Vander was scowling. Rhys' dark gaze was locked on her.

Haven's traitorous heart did a little tango in her chest.

Before she knew what was happening, Rhys went down on one knee in front of her.

She saw rage twist his handsome features. Then he shocked her by cupping her jaw, and pushing the ice pack away.

They'd never talked much. At Gia's parties, Haven purposely avoided him. He'd never touched her before, and she felt the warmth of him singe through her.

His eyes flashed. "It's going to be okay, baby."

Baby?

He stroked her cheekbone, those long fingers gentle.

Fighting for some control, Haven closed her hand over his wrist. She swallowed. "I—"

"Don't worry, Haven. I'm going to find the man who did this to you and make him regret it."

Her belly tightened. *Oh, God.* When was the last time anyone had looked out for her like this? She was certain no one had ever promised to hunt anyone down for her. Her gaze dropped to his lips.

He had amazingly shaped lips, a little fuller than such a tough man should have, framed by dark stubble.

There was a shift in his eyes and his face warmed. His fingers kept stroking her skin and she felt that caress all over.

Then she heard the click of heels moving at speed. Gia burst into the room.

"What the hell is going on?"

Haven jerked back from Rhys and his hypnotic touch. Damn, she'd been proven right—she was so weak where this man was concerned.

Gia hurried toward them. She was five-foot-four, with a curvy, little body, and a mass of dark, curly hair. As usual, she wore one of her power suits—short skirt, fitted jacket, and sky-high heels.

"Out of my way." Gia shouldered Rhys aside. When her friend got a look at Haven, her mouth twisted. "I'm going to *kill* them."

"Gia," Vander said. "The place is filled with cops. Maybe keep your plans for murder and vengeance quiet."

"Fix this." She pointed at Vander's chest, then at

Rhys. Then she turned and hugged Haven. "You're coming home with me."

"Gia—"

"No. No arguments." Gia held up her palm like a traffic cop. Haven had seen "the hand" before. It was pointless arguing.

Besides, she realized she didn't want to be alone. And the quicker she got away from Rhys' dark, far-too-perceptive gaze, the better.

Norcross Security
The Investigator
The Troubleshooter
The Specialist
The Bodyguard
The Hacker
The Powerbroker
The Detective
The Medic
The Protector
Also Available as Audiobooks!

PREVIEW: TREASURE HUNTER SECURITY

Want to learn more about *Treasure Hunter Security*? Check out the first book in the series, *Undiscovered*, Declan Ward's action-packed story.

One former Navy SEAL. One dedicated

archeologist. One secret map to a fabulous lost oasis.

Finding undiscovered treasures is always daring, dangerous, and deadly. Perfect for the men of Treasure Hunter Security. Former Navy SEAL Declan Ward is haunted by the demons of his past and throws everything he has into his security business—Treasure Hunter Security. Dangerous archeological digs – no problem. Daring expeditions – sure thing. Museum security for invaluable exhibits – easy. But on a simple dig in the Egyptian desert, he collides with a stubborn, smart archeologist, Dr. Layne Rush, and together they get swept into a deadly treasure hunt for a mythical lost oasis. When an evil from his past reappears, Declan vows to do anything to protect Layne.

Dr. Layne Rush is dedicated to building a successful career—a promise to the parents she lost far too young. But when her dig is plagued by strange accidents, targeted by a lethal black market antiquities ring, and artifacts are stolen, she is forced to turn to Treasure Hunter Security, and to the tough, sexy, and too-used-to-giving-orders Declan. Soon her organized dig morphs into a wild treasure hunt across the desert dunes.

Danger is hunting them every step of the way, and Layne and Declan must find a way to work together...to not only find the treasure but to survive.

Treasure Hunter Security
Undiscovered
Uncharted

Unexplored
Unfathomed
Untraveled
Unmapped
Unidentified
Undetected
Also Available as Audiobooks!

ALSO BY ANNA HACKETT

Fury Brothers

Fury

Keep

Also Available as Audiobooks!

Sentinel Security

Wolf

Hades

Striker

Steel

Excalibur

Hex

Also Available as Audiobooks!

Norcross Security

The Investigator

The Troubleshooter

The Specialist

The Bodyguard

The Hacker

The Powerbroker

The Detective

The Medic

The Protector

Also Available as Audiobooks!

Billionaire Heists

Stealing from Mr. Rich

Blackmailing Mr. Bossman

Hacking Mr. CEO

Also Available as Audiobooks!

Team 52

Mission: Her Protection

Mission: Her Rescue

Mission: Her Security

Mission: Her Defense

Mission: Her Safety

Mission: Her Freedom

Mission: Her Shield

Mission: Her Justice

Also Available as Audiobooks!

Treasure Hunter Security

Undiscovered

Uncharted

Unexplored

Unfathomed

Untraveled

Unmapped

Unidentified

Undetected

Also Available as Audiobooks!

Oronis Knights

Knightmaster

Knighthunter

Galactic Kings

Overlord

Emperor

Captain of the Guard

Conqueror

Also Available as Audiobooks!

Eon Warriors

Edge of Eon

Touch of Eon

Heart of Eon

Kiss of Eon

Mark of Eon

Claim of Eon

Storm of Eon

Soul of Eon

King of Eon

Also Available as Audiobooks!

Galactic Gladiators: House of Rone

Sentinel

Defender

Centurion

Paladin

Guard

Weapons Master

Also Available as Audiobooks!

Galactic Gladiators

Gladiator

Warrior

Hero

Protector

Champion

Barbarian

Beast

Rogue

Guardian

Cyborg

Imperator

Hunter

Also Available as Audiobooks!

Hell Squad

Marcus

Cruz

Gabe

Reed

Roth

Noah

Shaw

Holmes

Niko

Finn

Devlin

Theron

Hemi

Ash

Levi

Manu

Griff

Dom

Survivors

Tane

Also Available as Audiobooks!

The Anomaly Series

Time Thief

Mind Raider

Soul Stealer

Salvation

Anomaly Series Box Set

The Phoenix Adventures

Among Galactic Ruins

At Star's End

In the Devil's Nebula

On a Rogue Planet

Beneath a Trojan Moon

Beyond Galaxy's Edge

On a Cyborg Planet

Return to Dark Earth

On a Barbarian World

Lost in Barbarian Space

Through Uncharted Space

Crashed on an Ice World

Perma Series

Winter Fusion

A Galactic Holiday

Warriors of the Wind

Tempest

Storm & Seduction

Fury & Darkness

Standalone Titles

Savage Dragon

Hunter's Surrender

One Night with the Wolf

For more information visit www.annahackett.com

ABOUT THE AUTHOR

I'm a USA Today bestselling romance author who's passionate about ***fast-paced, emotion-filled*** contemporary romantic suspense and science fiction romance. I love writing about people overcoming unbeatable odds and achieving seemingly impossible goals. I like to believe it's possible for all of us to do the same.

I live in Australia with my own personal hero and two very busy, always-on-the-move sons.

For release dates, behind-the-scenes info, free books, and other fun stuff, sign up for the latest news here:

Website: www.annahackett.com